THE SORCERESS TRANSCENDENT

CASEY BLAIR

CHAPTER 1

H e had not come all this way to collapse without even knocking on her door.

Varius, very recently Legatus of the Aurelian Empire—so recently he was still bleeding from his sudden departure—reminded himself of that firmly, as breathing grew increasingly difficult, as blood pooled in his armor and dripped down his limbs, as he stumbled through the dark, ominous forest.

He had to believe he'd make it. He had no other choice now, his chances of surviving this reunion—if you could call it that when they'd never been on the same side of the war—merely astronomically bad instead of the definitively catastrophic future promised if he'd remained in the empire.

But he was as sure as he could be this was the direction he'd find her. When she'd first gone rogue, Varius had sifted through the rumors, and given how versed he'd become in searching for signs of her traps he'd sent soldiers to verify—

He sucked in a sharp breath, almost whited out from the pain, physical and emotional.

Don't think about your soldiers, Varius.

They are not yours anymore.

With effort, he put one foot in front of the other, disassociating himself from the pain of his body, his thoughts, trying to navigate the spindly branches that scratched him without losing his direction.

Almost there. Just a little longer.

He'd been telling himself that for miles now.

In truth, he'd been telling himself that for years.

Just one more battle, and maybe the war would finally be over.

Just one more death, one more tragedy as a family lost a son, as the sorceresses they fought wrought destruction matched only by what the empire could do with their sheer number of bodies, as the treacherous Aurelian patricians sent him into one more unwinnable situation. Just one more, and maybe he could grieve, or rest, or die.

But now it was just one more thicket to stumble through, and one way or another, he'd reach his destination.

It had better be soon. He knew how many wounds he was bleeding from. He hadn't made it across the border into Korossia uncontested, and he'd fought through his own people, surviving as he always did, even when everyone else died.

That had been hours ago.

The longer he went, the more it felt like the forest itself was trying to stop him. It wasn't—a sorceress had used that tactic on him years ago, so he knew what that felt like—but Varius caught himself tripping over branches and slipping on leaves more frequently. The daylight had faded, the spindly branches crowded out the moonlight, and he was tiring.

And then abruptly his path brightened. He looked up—he'd been watching the ground to stay on his feet—to find he'd emerged from the forest all at once, like it had been sheared off.

Whatever he'd been expecting from a renegade sorceress' lair, it wasn't this.

This wasn't a castle with intimidating spires, nor a hidden hovel tucked away in a corner.

Across the clearing was a house, with wild vines crawling up the sides. It looked like wood from the outside, and why not? No one was going to be able to burn down a sorceress' abode.

But Varius' eyes were drawn to the warm glow inside. Light, and the implication of heat—the thought pulled him forward, and he very deliberately pushed aside the thought that it looked like a *home*.

Only now that he was so close did his mind allow him to consider more than "just a little longer" and how badly this could go.

He was rapidly approaching the door of the one they now called the Sorceress Transcendent. The only sorceress who'd ever escaped from under the thumb of Korossia's impossibly powerful dictator, beating the Sorcerer Ascendant at his own game.

She'd done it with careful planning, and let's not forget mind-blowing destructive power. Which was what had made her, before she got herself out of the war, his most dangerous enemy.

He'd faced off against her countless times over the years, and whatever relationship he imagined they had—trading sallies and pointed, almost mischievous attacks across a battlefield, avoiding dealing death blows at each other when deniability was possible—it was imagined. Even if he thought they had both just tried to get their jobs done without killing the other, but also without veering into questions of treason while they went all-out against anyone else, they had still always been on opposite sides of the war.

The last time he'd seen her on the battlefield, she'd given him a cryptic warning that he'd apparently interpreted correctly to keep him and his legion clear of the vast destruction she'd wrought in order to go rogue.

But she'd also poisoned him first.

Not fatally, obviously, which was how she'd managed it; Varius knew her tells well enough to escape anything truly life-threatening, but it had still taken him a critical few days to recover any semblance of function.

He thought the poisoning had been an effort to protect him, to make sure the patricians couldn't order him into the field she'd been poised to raze.

But it also could have been to make absolutely sure he, the one Aurelian legatus who'd ever been able to keep up with her, couldn't interfere with her plan, and she'd taken him off the board the only way she'd been able to; the only way he'd let her.

Was it all a long con, which she had proved she was absolutely capable of, or did they really have a bizarre, twisted friendship?

If Varius was wrong, he'd die today.

And now he was going to, what, just knock on her door? Give her a chance to kill him when he couldn't put up even a token resistance, in case that had really been her goal all along?

And if it wasn't, he was going to show up already injured with nothing to offer her but problems she'd managed the impossible to leave behind? Hello, it's your favorite old enemy, let's have some tea and catch up before I bleed out on your floor?

This was a mistake.

Varius somehow slowed even further. Maybe all the branches he'd caught on in the forest had been his subconscious trying to convince him to make better choices.

Only now, out of the forest with no obstacles before him, did it feel like he was walking into a trap. Those vines up ahead could choke him, he was sure. And probably would.

But he was on a *path*, of all things, beautiful flat stones leading him on a lightly winding route through—gardens. Carefully cultivated, not a clearing after all. No wonder the trees had stopped so abruptly.

Even in the dark he could see the gardens were flourishing, which meant the sorceress who lived here had plenty of materials at hand to feed her spells and brandish them against him.

Not that she'd need to, in his current condition.

Varius reached the door.

It was huge, looming before him like it belonged to a castle instead of a cottage, with an ornate metal knocker. An appropriate hint of grandeur for any who dared approach a sorceress adept of the first tier.

There was also a mat at his feet, and in the light from the window it looked like it was woven with a floral design, more vines, and very clearly thorns, just like the ones framing the door.

The vines were probably poisonous, too, something she cultivated in her front yard. That would be just like her, to greet any visitors to her home with a cozy threat.

The thought obscurely centered him. This was probably a mistake, but under the circumstances he didn't have better options.

So Varius did what he always did. He steeled himself, and braced for impact.

Which is to say, he finally picked up the godscursed knocker, winced at his abused ribs, and knocked.

One breathless moment, where he suddenly realized she could simply not open the door to him—

And then she did.

The monstrous door opened partway, and there Theira stood, bathed in light.

Her black, wavy hair cascaded luxuriantly untamed around her, a dark contrast to her pale face. She wore a simple dress with a utility belt, a cozy mauve rather than the showy amethyst he associated with her on the battlefield, and for the first time he saw her without the bold makeup she favored.

Maybe she didn't bother because, for once, she didn't look tired.

Had he ever been this physically close to her? Varius couldn't recall. It seemed impossible, that he—they—could just be here. So close, one more step, and he could touch her, and not just in his dreams. He ached with the effort not to reach out, struck silent by the strange intimacy of the moment, her lips without paint, her beauty as wild as ever without adornment.

The vines around the door twisted, thorns pointing toward him in clear, unstated warning, but he barely noticed, so arrested by the sight of her and the sudden reality that she was really here, and *he* was here, that somehow they had both made it to this place together.

Surrounded as ever by barbs.

Into that silence, the Sorceress Transcendent spoke first.

"I was beginning to wonder," Theira said, cool amusement in her voice, "if you thought that this time for sure you would be able to simply stare me into submission."

It was the sound of her voice after all this time more than even the vision of her alive and well and free and gorgeous that almost undid him. His knees tried to buckle, and Varius caught himself.

Theira tracked the movement, and the thorny vines withdrew abruptly. She never missed anything, even if she didn't speak. How long had he stood at the door like a dumbass?

And now she also knew he was at her mercy, that he had no hidden strategy she needed to counter, that she could kill him at any time without worry. A first, for them. Varius might have been ashamed if he hadn't suspected she was nonplussed.

He stared at this sorceress, his once-best enemy, who waited with endless patience for him to get to the god-scursed point. He sucked in a breath to greet her politely and make his case, to explain and formally request her forbearance, but what made it out was:

"I had nowhere else to go."

The words dropped into the night like a stone in a pool.

Theira's deeply expressive eyes flickered, knowing.

Unimaginable, that his life had somehow come to this.

But the empire he had given his life and body and soul to had betrayed him—betrayed them all. No one there could protect him or anyone else any longer.

Varius had spent almost his whole life at war, and now it was only an enemy he could turn to.

Theira held his gaze for a long moment and then said, "You'd better come in."

He didn't register what she'd said until the door swung further open, letting out not just the light and warmth from inside, but revealing a clean entryway lined with life—overgrown potted plants, a rack for coats, a pair of gardening boots nestled in their own tray. A place where everything in her life fit, even if, like her own personality, it was always spilling out the seams.

He didn't fit. There wouldn't be a neat place for him where he wouldn't intrude on everything else.

This was her home. She'd gotten away, and now he was going to drag her back down with him.

Not that she had to let him.

When he didn't move, Theira finally asked, "Is there a problem?"

Varius was too tired, and possibly in shock, and couldn't put words together. Finally he blurted, "I'm bleeding."

"I see that," Theira said dryly, "and I also see no reason to patch you up out in the cold when I have a perfectly good house with all my materials inside."

She wanted to patch him up?

And did she sound defensive, or was he imagining it?

She continued, "Are you really going to show up at my doorstep and expect me to make myself uncomfortable for you?"

"No!" His denial was immediate, emphatic. Varius shook his head, and his gaze caught on the warm entryway behind her. "I just..."

The longing in his look, visibly overwhelmed, must have, embarrassingly, communicated itself without further words, because Theira just said, softly, "Oh." And then, dry once again: "After all these years, I promise I can clean up blood, Varius. There won't be any sign of stains."

The stains of his presence, of the war itself.

She understood. Of course she did. Her life had been as bloody as his, after all.

Still— "I'll clean it," he swore impulsively, his voice rough.

Her eyebrows lifted. "Well get in here then, and close the door behind you."

Varius took a deep breath, winced again at his fucking ribs and then himself because Theira's eyebrows abruptly drew down as she noticed.

He crossed the threshold.

And turned to lift his arm to close the door as she'd directed when it slammed shut behind him with worrying speed and force.

He was closed in her lair now.

His heart thumped.

Varius turned back to regard her cautiously.

Theira had already turned away and wasn't waiting on him.

"Don't puncture a lung on my account," she said coolly, "especially when I've already said I'd patch you up. I'm confident you don't need to add more injuries to my workload. This way."

As if in a dream, Varius followed her. The house was clean—somehow he'd always imagined she would be messy—and the walls were bare. But when they got to the kitchen, Varius stopped suddenly enough to make himself wince as he took it all in.

Plants bloomed on shelves around the room, and others crowded among all manner of bottles and jars. This space, too, was clean, but overflowing. This was a place where she spent time, let herself flow into the space around her.

And Varius was totally unprepared for how relieved he was to see it. The signs of life, of flourishing, and of *her*, in this cozy, overflowing kitchen.

"Varius." He shivered at the sound of his name in her rich voice and looked up; Theira pointed at a chair. "Sit down before you fall down."

The chair looked so soft and plush he was worried he wouldn't get out of it once he got in. Not what he would have expected in an Aurelian kitchen, but after all she'd been through, maybe she'd decided she deserved comfort wherever she could find it. Varius certainly wasn't going to gainsay that.

He wanted to protest he'd stain it with blood, but she wouldn't think well of him wasting her time with the same argument twice. She was a sorceress adept of the first tier; her cushions wouldn't stay blood-soaked unless she wanted them to.

He grunted as he settled himself carefully down, his breath hissing out when his armor settled on him. He almost sprang back up, but then Theira was there, kneeling before him.

His heart thumped again.

She frowned at his armor, then looked up at him through her lashes full of teasing challenge.

Varius could feel his blood pounding in his veins as, with a smirk, Theira raised one finger, holding his gaze, then drew it down in a careful line against his chest.

How he wished he could feel that finger.

His armor crumbled off him like she'd sliced through it at the nonexistent seams.

Varius knew his eyes would be darkening. It was probably for the best he was so exhausted she wouldn't be able to see visible evidence of his lust surging in response to her.

Still, he held himself unmoving, waiting for her. Not just because he'd put himself in her copious power out of desperation, but because he couldn't imagine what he could offer her, now or ever.

No, that wasn't true. He knew cursed well there was nothing.

But they'd been watching each other, teasing, challenging, for years across battlefields, and he'd never been sure if he was the only one who felt, who *dreamed,* of more.

Theira was probably just playing with him, and that was fair, all things considered.

But she had opened the door.

Varius looked like a ghost of himself.

Theira had always found him beautiful, like he'd emerged from the earth itself. Skin bronzed from the sun, deep brown hair, sturdy as a rock and just as unmovable. When you faced him across the battlefield, you knew he'd dig in and dig deep and it would require heroic force to move him.

Something had moved him today.

Varius had been looking more and more tired as the years went by. At some point she'd realized he was her reflection, and if she was going to save herself, it would have to be soon.

He'd apparently missed his cut-off date—or maybe that was why he was here.

Here, in her house.

He'd come to her, put himself where she could reach him, touch him, and he'd done it on purpose.

Theira had lived for years under the terrible scrutiny of the most powerful sorcerer in the world, so she didn't fidget as she made him a cup of tea and tried not to worry about what he thought of her house.

He was silent, which was probably because he was on his last legs and not because he was judging her. For escaping, or for managing to and living in a place that looked like this. What did she know of normal houses, growing up in the vicious training halls in the bowels under Castle Korossia?

Varius probably had a warm, earthy kitchen back at his hometown, not overflowing with sorcerous experiments, and with people who were soft and gentle and knew how to comfort and relax rather than command him into a chair and strip him.

Then again. He was here. If he had that kitchen to go to in the Aurelian Empire, it wasn't one with a sorceress who could protect herself—and him.

And he probably didn't have it, or he wouldn't have looked so godscursed tired all the time.

Grabbing a stack of towels, Theira crossed back to the table and set the mug down.

"Let's see what we've got," she said briskly to disguise how her thoughts clamored that she was finally, after so many imaginings, going to touch his body with her own two hands—the man was bleeding, for Gaia's sake.

She brought a towel to the first clear source of blood on his arm.

Varius' frankly unreasonable abs flexed as he braced against the touch on his open wound.

She glared at him until he blinked in apparent confusion as she wiped him off.

"Of course it won't hurt for me to clean off the blood," Theira said impatiently. "I'm a *sorceress.*"

Though she could make it hurt if she wanted to, and maybe that was what really bothered her—that he might assume pain was all he could expect from her.

Varius' eyes were dark as he focused on her with thrilling intensity and he said gruffly, "I know."

She had enough control not to shiver.

Of all people, he knew.

And he was here, letting her use sorcery on him without *comment,* let alone protest, which spoke to either a deep level of trust in someone who'd nearly killed him more than once, or profound desperation.

Theira needed to know which.

For now, she *hmmm*ed and turned back to her task of cleaning him enough to take stock of his wounds, and maybe also his muscles for future daydreaming.

Varius directed her to the root of his injuries more than once, and she kept her expression professional. She'd offered to patch him up and he was taking her at her word, and maybe that shouldn't mean so much, but it did.

No one ever took someone like her at face value.

She'd worked hard for that, in fact, and now she reaped what she'd sown.

Through it all, after that initial instinctual tightening, Varius held himself impossibly still. The armor had protected his vital organs, but he definitely had some broken ribs from whatever he'd faced to get all the way here—and he'd come on foot, which meant he'd been running for *hours* like this.

Even without her movements adding to his pain, this had to be excruciating, but he was always *so* controlled.

Then again, maybe he was just repulsed by her and keeping it to himself until she'd fixed him.

Or maybe it was something else.

Theira stepped back. "Start drinking the tea. I'll get some salves."

She was already across the room before Varius asked, "What's in it?"

She almost sagged in relief. Thank Gaia, something other than blind obedience. He wasn't dead yet.

Just broken.

Without missing a beat, Theira answered, "Mind control potion."

A faint huff. She glanced back over her shoulder as Varius met her gaze and deliberately took a sip.

"Always such a liar," he murmured. Fondly—or was that her imagination? It wasn't as though Theira had any experience relating to another person honestly. She'd have to decide—later.

Theira sniffed, turning back to her shelves so she didn't have to care what her face did as she enjoyed the spark she always felt playing with him. "I could brew a mind control potion if I wanted."

"Far be it from me to question your skill."

No, he knew that all too well.

Abruptly she said, "It's for rejuvenation, with a little added for pain management. It'll help you heal faster to get back in the game."

Varius didn't answer.

When she looked back, he didn't look encouraged—his whole body sagged.

Her heart clenched. He might have been her enemy once, but that was not a good sign.

Looking forward to sparring with him had once been the only light that kept her going. If he didn't want to fight, was there anything left between them? Since her escape she had thoroughly demonstrated she didn't know how to be a light for anyone else.

But he was here under her grace and knew it, so maybe she could try the direct approach and just ask what in Gaia's name he needed from her. How novel.

Potion bottles in hand, Theira returned to his side, set them down, and looked him hard in the eye. "Are you going to tell me what happened?"

"They'll follow me," Varius whispered. "I shouldn't have brought you into this."

Oh for Gaia's sake, what a fucking martyr. "I promise I was perfectly capable of not opening my door."

Varius suddenly smiled faintly, and it was like the whole room grew warmer. *Oof.*

"*Were* you capable of not opening the door?" he asked her. *Teased* her. "Not knowing what I was here for?"

Ha. He had her there.

In a way, he knew her better than anyone. That was dangerous.

But part of the whole point of leaving was that she didn't have to care about that anymore. At least, not the way she had.

"You're on my turf," Theira reminded him. "I can maneuver you into a truth spell any time I want. Tell me."

The light faded from his gaze, and she ached with regret at the loss.

Finally, eyes closed as if he couldn't bear to look at his words, Varius ground out, "Sobanus ordered me to march on the city."

It took Theira a moment to realize he didn't mean Korossia; he meant one of the Aurelian Empire's *own* cities.

Well, that certainly explained what had gotten Varius moving. He not only would never have done it, he wouldn't have stood for it. His loyalty was to his people, not their aristocratic oligarchs, and anyone on either side of the border knew it.

"There's been more unrest," Varius said. "The empire calls more and more people, younger every year, to fight in a war with no end in sight. There are fewer to work the fields, to make the boots and arrows. We salvage them from the dead. I did what I could to protect rebels who protested, getting them out of jail, paying fines so some could stay home. Sending kids to fight is bad enough. The patricians expect me to murder them? I can't. I *won't*."

Theira squeezed more of one salve onto her hands and worked it into the monstrous muscle of his arm. "Caius Sobanus is a known asshole. Do you think he really expected you to?"

Varius was silent a moment. "I don't know. It was obviously a loyalty test, but I've never disobeyed direct orders like that before. If he wanted me out of his way, he could have just fired me for not managing to win their war yet." He sighed. "But Sobanus *is* an asshole, and he wouldn't miss a chance to stick a knife in my ribs first."

"It may be more than that," Theira commented. "Sobanus isn't stupid. Firing the most successful legatus? People would have never stood for it, and if he thinks the rebels might see you as a figurehead, the only way to get rid of you is to kill you—and to get your own soldiers to do it so you're not martyred. He'll have told them something different about why you left."

Varius grunted. "Yeah. That much was clear."

Sorceresses worked alone. She'd never been responsible for soldiers, but she knew how seriously he took his responsibility to defend them, and having to kill them in order to escape would have cracked something in him. No wonder the fight had gone out of him. "I'm sorry you had to face them like that."

At this point Theira had finished usefully working a potion into Varius' ribcage and was just massaging the area, feeling the play of his ridiculous muscles under her hands.

"Me too," Varius said softly. "But it's better than it could have been. Sobanus knew I'd avoid the barracks, but expected me to go to ground in the city. He didn't think I had anywhere to go."

It took Theira a moment to realize he'd looked down and was now just watching her touch him. His feet were firmly planted on the floor, and she was kneeling between his legs.

His eyes as he watched her were dark, glittering.

She grinned up at him, as if it were not embarrassing to be caught distracted by the realness of him, *here*, when he'd just been forced to flee for his life.

"You're half naked in my kitchen and I can finally satisfy my curiosity," Theira said with a shrug.

Varius looked faintly stunned.

Oh no. Had she misread after all? She didn't have anything like his charm and ease with people.

Maybe that was too personal. She didn't want to destroy the surreal truce they had going, so she tried one more time to make it into more of a joke.

"Any wounds that would justify taking your pants off?"

Silence.

On further reflection, if her goal was to set him at ease, that may not have been the joke to do it.

Theira shriveled internally as she forced herself to sit back to keep him from being uncomfortable here in a place he came to only because he had no other options—*more* uncomfortable—because she wasn't sure she could bear it if someone finally came to her for help and then she was the reason they fled.

She was just about to get to her feet when Varius said, his voice dry and very, very rough, "Unless you have a rejuvenation potion with a little more kick, I don't think you'll be impressed with anything in my pants tonight."

Theira kept her expression one of mild amusement but thought he could probably see the brightness in her eyes. Unreasonable, for her heart to soar like this, from so little—but he was *playing*, despite the devastation made of his life in the last day, and with *her*, when he knew better than anyone what she could do.

She hadn't misread him, or made him uncomfortable. At least, not so much that he was going to flee from her.

Then again, given what it had taken to get him to move, he would withstand a lot of discomfort if he thought he had to.

Maybe she didn't deserve to have nice things after all she'd done, but that wasn't how she wanted him.

Theira smiled, so he wouldn't think *she* was fleeing, and withdrew back to the kitchen. "After this healing, you're going to sleep like a rock anyway."

"Not magical sleep?" Varius asked. "You know they'll come for me, I don't want you—"

"Varius. Why did you come here?"

A beat.

Theira crossed back to him and leaned down, her eyes right in front of his.

And then with heat in his voice, Varius said, "Because if anyone can get the better of them, it's you."

Theira's smile was slow and feral.

It was so nice to be appreciated without the cowering.

She purred, "And it will be my pleasure."

The fire in him faded, and his shoulders slumped. "But what can be done? They won't give up. This war will go on forever."

She eyed him critically. A little hopelessness after the day he'd had was entirely justified, but that wasn't how she wanted him, either.

And she didn't think it was what he wanted.

So the Sorceress Transcendent just said, "Sleep. We'll talk about it tomorrow."

CHAPTER 2

Varius woke slowly. It had been so long since he'd woken naturally that he panicked slightly thinking he'd been drugged, shoving upwards in bed. But that bit of adrenaline was enough to clear his head, and he felt—fine, actually.

Given the shape he'd been in, that was practically a miracle. He felt a stab of envy for the power of sorcerous healing.

Then his mind flashed back to Theira's hands on him as part of that healing, and his stomach muscles tightened involuntarily.

That had really happened. Varius felt the blood rushing down to his groin at the mere memory.

So, that was working again, too. He wasn't sure if he should be grateful for that, given how much she'd be able to see.

Varius had been dreaming of her for years, and the little taste he'd had only fired his imagination more.

He needed to be careful, because as the whole empire knew, he was not a man who gave himself by halves. She might only have a use for his body.

Then again, maybe that was all he could hope for, now.

Irritated with his own internal whining, Varius shook his head and scooted to the edge of the bed, looking around for the first time.

Theira had been right—once she'd stopped working on him, she'd barely had time to explain that the potions she'd applied pulled from his own energy to speed his healing before he'd nearly dropped asleep in the chair. She'd led him to this room, and he'd fallen face first onto the bed and been out in seconds.

He was a poor guest. He'd fix that today.

In the light of day, he took in the room. All the furniture here—bed, desk and chair, shelves—was wood, too, which had to be on purpose—he'd heard Castle Korossia was all gray rock. This room had splashes of color—a green blanket, a blue rug. The shelves were full of books on various crafts—woodworking, pottery—and some small plants.

It made a solid effort at coziness, with all the items a guest might need, but nothing that felt like it carried a sense of Theira's self. Even the plants were too well contained for her. It all gave Varius the impression that she didn't actually know what a feeling of "home" meant.

And why should she? Potential sorceresses were taken from their families as children and brought to the castle to fight for their lives, pitted against each other, and only the most ruthless made it to adulthood.

Even if Theira knew what a house was supposed to look like, she couldn't know what it felt like—and she wouldn't expose herself to someone who was a stranger in her life. And it was all impersonal, clearly intended for a guest.

Which made him wonder: What kind of guests did she receive here?

Varius shook his head at the bolt of jealousy the thought caused. Whoever her friends were, he wasn't going to convince Theira he should count among the number of people she could trust by lying in bed all day.

He didn't deserve to, anyway. He was the one who had brought the war back to her door.

Varius found a neat pile of clothes that turned out to fit him perfectly. He probably shouldn't be surprised, given how close a look she'd gotten yesterday.

Definitely the most enjoyable tailoring session he could recall.

He appreciated the thought, even as taking off his clothes to change shocked emotion into him. Like he was shucking off the last of the empire's hold on him.

Choosing a sorceress.

Starting fresh.

Which reminded him that despite his promise yesterday he hadn't cleaned the floor for her.

Selfishly, he hoped she'd left it, so he could make good on that today.

Once he was as clean and ready as he was getting, he took a breath and opened the door.

Time to start doing something besides dragging Theira down with him.

Varius followed the sound of jars opening and a sizzling pan back to the kitchen.

The walls on his way were all bare, too.

Only the kitchen was different. Like Theira couldn't help overflowing into any space she spent time in.

Or maybe she'd painstakingly drawn herself out of the shell she'd had to build for herself in Korossia.

"Take a seat," Theira said without turning to look at him. "Breakfast is almost ready."

In a kind of daze yet again, Varius brought himself to the same chair he'd occupied yesterday. No blood anywhere.

And the Sorceress Transcendent was cooking for him.

"Can I help?" Varius asked.

Theira froze.

Briefly, only a second before she got a hold of herself, but it was enough to make him feel like an asshole for not offering sooner.

And to make him angry that apparently a person offering to help her was so godscursed rare the very idea
shocked her into a visible reaction.

Whoever her guests were, they didn't deserve any
more of her than that room gave.

"Thank you, but I'm just about finished," Theira said.

Varius looked around. Sure enough, there was no trace
he'd come through here yesterday. "You cleaned up after
me."

"I did promise you I could handle a few stains."
So she had.

"Did you expect me to just leave dirt on my floor?" she
asked, carrying a plate of food and a steaming mug to the
table.

Varius stared at her, heart thumping in familiar excite-
ment at the sight of her like the sorceress he remem-
bered, bright red lips and dark eyeshadow and highlight-
ed cheeks, the magical purple dress and elegant, deadly
belt.

She was dressed to kill.

She set the food and tea in front of him like a godscursed restaurant server and turned to leave.

Varius surged to his feet without even looking at the
food. "Where can I find us flatware?"

Theira blinked. Blinked twice.

"That drawer." She pointed. "Napkins in that one."

Varius nodded like he'd been given marching orders and snapped to it. Theira watched him for a moment before returning to her station and dishing her own food.

Varius picked the first napkins and flatware out of the drawers, both swirled with vines, and carried them back and distributed them as Theira sat down with her own food.

"Thank you," she said, like she wasn't sure what to make of this.

"Thank *you*," Varius said, sitting down again, feeling both slightly better for having done *something* but also like anger was an itch under his skin. He'd done *nothing*. "The food looks wonderful."

And it did. His plate was piled high with an omelet full of vegetables, sausage, fruit, toast.

"I was hardly going to let you starve after inviting you in."

Varius took a sip of tea first before saying, "And what an easy way to dose me with a potion, too."

Theira smiled. "Too easy, no challenge. It's not as if I want you to decide you need to forage for yourself in my garden."

Varius snorted. "I'd probably kill myself trying."

"It's not *all* poisonous," she said primly.

He grinned. "In the interest of inspiring you to greater challenge, I admit I probably couldn't tell."

She rolled her eyes. "Soldiers. If you can't stab with it, it's not worth learning about."

He wasn't a soldier anymore. But rather than dwell on that he said, "You're not going to sit there and tell me you can't grow a perfectly normal looking plant that would actually kill me."

Theira smiled like a blow to his chest. "No, I'm not."

Varius felt unreasonably pleased with himself for getting that smile out of her.

She should smile that wickedly all the time, and maybe that was one thing he could do for her.

"I didn't get a good look last night, but it looks like your gardens are expansive and flourishing," Varius said. "Do you grow your own food, along with everything else?"

"Mostly."

"Is that so you'll always know what's poisonous?"

Theira rolled her eyes again, but, he thought, fondly. "As if I couldn't tell if someone else tried to poison me? Please. No, it's mostly convenience."

"Ah. You are pretty far from anything out here." Sausage would keep, but she must use sorcery for the eggs. Had she broken out a few from a precious stash so he could eat something familiar?

Then again, for all he knew he was eating eggs of something other than a chicken that she kept in her basement.

Another thought struck him. "Has the Sorcerer Ascendant pressured people to not sell you food?"

Theira shook her head. "No need. I'm not going to put people in any more danger to help me. The people who built my house are protected, but if I started doing that commonly Tychon would make a point of... challenging that protection."

And the Sorcerer Ascendant was the one person alive who could definitely break it.

Varius frowned, wondering anew about that guest room. But he said, "You said 'mostly'. What else is it?"

Theira considered him for a moment, then shrugged as if it didn't matter. "I like growing things."

The simple statement hit him like a punch in the gut.

Gods. He knew how much she reveled in sorcerous destruction, and he'd be lying if he said he himself didn't take satisfaction in knowing he'd hit an opponent just right to take them out.

But there was another side of her, too, that she was trying to give space to in this house.

She liked growing things.

If he didn't have to kill for the empire, what would he do?

He'd barely considered the question before; it was an impossibility.

Theira had a garden, though, and it was flourishing.

But her house was empty.

"All those craft books in the guest room," Varius said slowly. "Are they for you?"

"Yes, all the guest rooms have books like that. I've hardly read them all, but I thought it was better to have them ready in case the need arises."

"Wait. How many guest rooms do you have? Do you have that many guests out here?"

For all his wondering about her other guests, it was only in this moment that Varius realized he might not be the only one in the house with her.

But Theira's careful expression cut that line of thought off as she said quietly, "You're my first."

Oh. *Oh.*

His heart ached for her as he realized all at once. "You thought, after you escaped, that others might come to you."

Theira sighed, pushing the food around on her plate. Varius made a point of taking a big bite, not letting her effort for him go unappreciated or to waste.

"Silly, in retrospect," she said. "Tychon's probably made it even harder for anyone to take actions without his oversight, given what I managed. And none of them has any reason to believe they might trust me—all they know is that I'm powerful, clever, and don't want to live under the Sorcerer Ascendant. But that describes almost all of them. But if someone did think to try…"

That's why she had guest rooms. Spare clothes, even.

But the only one who'd thought to come to her was her enemy.

Had she been as desperate to open the door to someone, anyone, as he'd been to have a door open to him?

Varius didn't want her to think of him as just another supplicant.

"How *did* you manage to get away?" he asked. "I knew not to believe the official story, but what actually happened was never totally clear."

Theira smiled a little. "After that first battle—"

Her smile died abruptly, because while it hadn't been her first battle by any stretch, she didn't need to specify which one she meant. Even among sorceresses, Theira was known for her epic destructive capabilities, but at that one she'd taken it to another level.

Varius had been fighting another sorcerer at the time and was called over to support—he was the only general who reliably survived Theira. He didn't know what traps his jackass colleague had missed and whether he might have caught them, but by the time he'd been within miles of the site, it had already been over. His people had just seen the explosions in the sky.

He'd known some of the kids who'd died that day, and he was sad for them. But Theira had been as trapped in the war as they were, and compared to some of her brethren, at least her sorcerous attacks weren't cruel. She didn't torture those kids; they just died. She didn't spread destruction indiscriminately or horrifically; she just killed. Precisely, terrifyingly. And if those kids hadn't died that day under the orders of that particular jackass, it still would have come at someone else's hands.

They were all of them trapped.

So after an awkward pause where Theira seemed to be debating what to say after that, Varius just nodded.

Apparently deciding he didn't need her to say any more about it, she continued, "That was the first decisive victory on either side in years. The Sorcerer Ascendant awarded me one of the largest jewels in Korossia's collection, only a step down from the Crown Jewel itself."

An impressive statement. While sorceresses could store and draw power from all manner of jewels—from all natural resources, though gemstones were special—Korossia's Crown Jewel was unique. It held incomparable power and could only be accessed by the person who bound themself to it—and it could also only bind to the one who killed the prior bearer.

That was the true source of a Sorcerer Ascendant's power: access to the largest pool of magic available that no one else could use. It's what made them nearly impossible to kill, even for a sorceress of Theira's experience. Not to mention the fact that the Ascendant would have managed the same feat meant they were invariably both shrewd *and* powerful.

Theira continued, "I thanked Tychon graciously, turned around, and broke it into a thousand tiny jewels I could actually convert into capital."

Varius barked a laugh despite himself. Of course she had.

But that had been years earlier. "You were building this all that time?"

"I was having it built," Theira corrected. "What does a sorceress know about building?"

What indeed.

"I hired experts and paid for materials, I made it worth their while, and I hid the whole thing from under Tychon's nose. You may have noticed after that battle—"

"Your tactics turned to precision. Effective, but not dramatic. I'd wondered where your power was really going, but I thought we'd found out."

When, a year later, she'd managed a *second* dramatic victory.

Varius hadn't been at that one either. He'd always been hesitant to seriously consider that his absence from both was on purpose as wishful thinking and arrogance.

But he was wondering again now.

"Everyone knows I'm a long-term planner," Theira said, "so after my first decisive victory wasn't immediately followed by a second, I bought myself time at court because everyone who believed it was possible for me to replicate that success also believed I needed time to work toward a bigger one."

"Your long-term planning becomes part of the long-term plan," Varius remarked dryly.

Theira flashed him a grin. "Indeed. It took as long as it did because I had to keep them from finding out what I was actually doing. But when I managed it, Tychon was in a difficult position. He'd already rewarded me with the biggest jewel he could part with, and since I'd delivered both a second victory, and a bigger one, he had to top the previous reward. So he offered me a boon. And I took it."

It took Varius a second. "You just resigned? At court, to his face?"

Theira's grin grew wicked. "Indeed," she said again, this time in a lower voice that _did things_ to his now-responsive loins. "And since the Sorcerer Ascendant knew I wouldn't dare if I didn't believe, in that moment, that I could back it up, he let me go, fully intending to make me pay later once he'd worked out what I'd planned."

"And did he?"

"No. I didn't have anything there."

Varius stared, and then started laughing helplessly. "You beautiful liar. You spent years on a reputation to make him believe it long enough for you to get somewhere you _did_ have spells ready."

An insane risk.

More insane than running away to the door of your lifelong enemy.

She'd *planned* her gamble, and her escape, and made it.

Theira's eyes were bright over her mug of tea. "And now here I am."

And then the light in her eyes faded.

Here she was, in an empty house. Full of books about crafts just in case she ever needed to learn something, because she couldn't count on anyone helping her. Varius could come to her, but where could *she* go?

To him.

The thought surged through him with the force of an avalanche.

She'd worked, and she'd tried, and somehow she'd still found herself in a situation where she'd escaped but was still trapped. Where no one took care of her, and she didn't even expect it.

He wanted her to believe that she should expect it.

And that from him, she could.

"Here you are," Varius echoed, and drained his tea without breaking eye contact.

Let her see that he wasn't afraid of who she was, and that he'd take her as she was.

"Let me clean up," he told her.

Theira waved him off. "Not necessary. I can—"

"I know you *can*," Varius practically growled.

She blinked at him, apparently nonplussed.

And then her head whipped around.

To the door.

Theira stood slowly, rising to her full height, and Varius watched her bearing transform her from a woman eating breakfast to a goddess ready for battle.

Gods curse it. He'd known they'd come, but here in Theira's kitchen he'd allowed himself to begin to hope they'd have more time.

She hadn't, he realized now.

That's why she was dressed for war.

"Well, well," the Sorceress Transcendent purred. "We have company."

Theira strode to the entryway, donning her work boots, casting a quick illusion so they matched her Battle Sorceress look, and flinging a cloak over her shoulders for dramatics.

Her cutthroat upbringing had duly impressed upon her how image created a perception of power, and she used every advantage she had.

"Wait." Varius followed her. "They're here for me."

"Of course they are." Theira raised her eyebrows. "Are you in any condition to fight off a sorcerous task force alone?"

She didn't want him to focus on what he couldn't do now that he'd gone rogue, but they didn't have time for a long discussion here.

He stilled. "Sorcerous? Not Aurelian?"

Theira shrugged. "You're a popular man."

The legions he'd led had done more damage to Korossia and killed more sorceresses than any single other person in the empire. Caius Sobanus couldn't possibly want him deader than Korossia did.

Varius cast her a look that was part amusement, part annoyance. "I suppose it's easier for sorceresses to get here than for an Aurelian Empire cohort to cross the border unmolested."

"Indeed. And Varius." His gaze focused on hers as she held his stare. "You are my guest here. Allow me to resolve this small matter for you."

Something passed through his gaze, and she hoped it wasn't pity. Theira wanted to seem *less* desperate than she'd sounded over breakfast, not more.

She was retired, not broken. She could be all of herself now.

She hoped.

Then Varius smiled, and her whole body zinged with awareness.

"Well, far be it from me to keep you back from some light exercise," he murmured. "Yell if I can help you dig some graves once you're finished."

Theira relaxed.

He still had faith in her.

She smirked at him before turning to the door.

She didn't have long to wait until a woman called, "Former First-Tier Adept Theira! You are harboring a fugitive guilty of the highest crimes against Korossia. I am here to remove this burden from you. You may turn him over at once."

Not even a knock. Her own former enemy had been more polite.

And if that was how Korossia was beginning this encounter, there was only one way for it to go.

"See?" Theira glanced over her shoulder. "The *highest* crimes. So famous."

Varius rolled his eyes. "You know what they say, murder is a fast way to make friends." She held in a laugh. "Would you like me visible in the background for this?"

Theira's chest eased further. As confident as she was, this challenge was the first big step for both of them in what came next, and she wasn't sure where Varius stood. She didn't think *he* knew where he stood, because he hadn't begun to consider what could be possible.

He wasn't with her. Not yet.

But he wasn't working against her anymore. He was *on her side*. And that mattered more than she wanted to admit.

So she would take this step for both of them, and give him some reason to hope.

Her heart pounded in anticipation. She'd recognized the voice leading the task force, too, and it simplified things. Kryseia had no interest in being saved.

"Out of sight," Theira said, "but feel free to watch the show. Toss me that mug?"

Varius sketched a bow with good humor and retreated. An empty mug sailed her way, and she caught it with magic.

Then Theira threw open the door, slamming it against her house with a bang, and advanced onto her doorstep.

One first-tier adept, with a passel of lower-tier sorcerers. The most skilled sorceresses worked alone, but they would know it would take more than one to take her down on her own turf if it came to that.

And oh, it would come to that.

"Hello, Kryseia," Theira addressed the sorceress in charge of this expedition, pretending to take a sip of tea. "Lovely weather in my garden today, don't you think?"

Kryseia's ice blue eyes flickered at the reminder that she stood on Theira's prepared ground.

Or maybe it was at her disrespect.

Kryseia tossed her elaborately and immaculately styled platinum hair, such a contrast to Theira's wild dark locks streaming around her. "My title is First-Tier Adept Kryseia."

"Likewise mine," Theira said idly. "Unless you mean to suggest that having more time to myself has worsened my skill?"

Kryseia glared, but none of the others even exchanged glances; they had chosen to obey Kryseia without question, which meant there was nothing Theira could do for them. Kryseia had long since attached her star to orbiting the Sorcerer Ascendant Tychon', had probably volunteered for this mission to recover her dignity after Theira had shown her up on the battlefield not once, but twice.

"I'm not here to exchange pleasantries with you, the so-called *Sorceress Transcendent*, who abandoned her duty," Kryseia declared. "We know you're holding the former legatus Varius Aurelian. Bring him out, and we'll be on our way out of your life once more."

That title. It probably didn't bode well for Theira, if even the Sorcerer Ascendant's top lackeys were using it. Kryseia's bitterness was a bigger surprise but easily accounted for by the fact that Theira had any title that she didn't.

Theira waited for Kryseia to finish.

Then she calmly took another mock-sip of tea, drawing it out.

Two of the lower-tier sorcerers broke their stare without moving, gazes flicking around for activity.

Wise. Much too late, but admirable instincts.

Kryseia ground her teeth.

"You don't call, you don't write, and you show up at my doorstep making demands," Theira said. "I'm retired, Kryseia. And even if I weren't, I don't take orders from you."

That undeniable refusal was the signal Kryseia's team was evidently waiting for. They began to fan out, their spells activating.

Theira had to give Kryseia credit though; for all her personal dislike, she had to know how this could go, and she gave it one last shot.

No doubt on the chance it might distract her, because Kryseia, too, would have learned to use every possible advantage.

"You don't want to do this, Theira," Kryseia said, her voice all false sympathy, with no effort to disguise her condescension. "You know as well as anyone what Varius has done to Korossia. We can take him off your hands, and you can keep your little retirement and never have to fight again. This doesn't have to be your problem."

Theira smiled.

And without moving slammed the door shut behind her.

"I believe there has been a misunderstanding, Kryseia," Theira said gently. "You seem to be under the impression that I have lost my taste for battle."

Vines erupted out of the ground, grabbing a portion of Kryseia's party who'd begun casting at her house and snapping their necks in an instant.

She grinned widely at Kryseia.

"I assure you," Theira purred, her blood singing, "this is not the case."

Kryseia's eyes went wide, but she didn't miss a beat, yelling orders and snapping a hand out in the same moment to fire a blast of sheer power at Theira. Her own power, even, no doubt to buy time to finish getting other spells into place.

Had Theira been unprepared, this would have been very impressive. But no first-tier adept, and Theira least of all, was ever that unprepared.

Not to mention they were on Theira's ground.

Kryseia's blast bounced off her.

Theira strolled forward, her advance activating enchantments with each step, her hair rising to crackle around her, electrified by her power.

Strangled screams echoed in the background as the protections she'd placed on her house reacted violently to their not-quite-subtle-enough intrusions, as beautiful flowers' poisonous gas choked off the strike team's air, as the roots under her garden dragged them beneath to feed on.

She paid them no mind. Her garden needed no further guidance from her for sorcerers of their caliber. They weren't even a distraction from the real battle before her.

Theira reached for the power of her garden, and threw it against Kryseia's next assault.

Their eyes met, and Theira knew this was what Kryseia had wanted.

Her, too.

She was glad to no longer be part of the endless, stupid, horrible war.

She did sometimes miss the freedom of wreaking rampant destruction.

Kryseia flung spell after spell at her, and Theira deflected every sally without apparent effort, driving Kryseia back step by step.

She'd missed this, too. The matching of power and wits against someone who could stand against her.

But Kryseia, for all her sorcery, was no Varius.

Kryseia could use the life force of the garden, too, but not as efficiently. Theira knew every plant, its location and potential.

She knew every spell she'd woven into the ground.

Kryseia's breath came increasingly fast as she struggled under Theira's assault. Her rhythm didn't break, but Theira could see her casting around for inspiration, for power, for something that could turn the tide.

Theira almost didn't recognize the feint for what it was, until the mug she still carried shattered in her hand.

Kryseia grinned triumphantly.

A piece of her new home, new life, broken in an instant act of malice. A challenge, that Theira could not, in fact, protect herself or anyone else.

Kryseia's power closed around her. She'd attempted to break Theira's flow, and she'd succeeded.

But Theira reached for the wild flame of her own power and exploded it outward.

"Congratulations," she told the sorceress who'd jumped clear but now watched her warily; Theira was known for not committing her own power. "You have my full attention."

And then Theira stopped playing.

Kryseia cast furiously, but it was no use against Theira actually tapping into her own power along with the garden.

It was a matter of moments before she'd shepherded Kryseia just where she wanted her: a spell laid in advance. Once she stepped into the circle, poisonous vines snaked around her ankles and thorns bit through her spells and skin, immobilizing her.

In moments she'd be unable to move at all—not a muscle, certainly. But not her lungs, either, or her heart.

She could have still cast, except Theira also pressed her own shroud of power around Kyrseia like a smothering pillow.

It was done, without so much as an explosion to mark her passing, and from Kryseia's furious gaze, she knew it. She would fade quietly out of this world with nothing to show for it. But first—

"You would do all this," she hissed, "for a man? An Aurelian worm who's killed scores of us?"

Which part of Varius offended her most? It didn't matter.

"This is my house," Theira said gently. "This is my ground. Here you are supplicant, not master. I will do what I wish, and you cannot force me."

"So if I'd said 'pretty please will you do this favor to all your sisters', you'd have said yes?" Kryseia sneered.

The expression faltered as she lost control of her facial muscles.

Theira smiled. "Of course not."

And then she stabbed Kryseia through the heart with a shard of the broken mug.

No need to draw it out when the fun was done. Now all that was left was clean-up.

Kryseia's wide eyes met hers, and Theira saw mania there. "He'll come for you," she gasped. "You'll have no peace now."

So that was what Kryseia was doing here. She must have lost too much influence at court after Theira's success in spite of the Sorcerer Ascendant. She could reclaim her status only by beating her.

And failing that, at least she'd ensured Theira's downfall.

Theira could have let Kryseia die believing she could rest easy, that even if it had gone like this, she'd won.

Instead she leaned forward and whispered in Kryseia's ear, "I'm counting on it."

CHAPTER 3

Varius met Theira at the door with a grin. "It's more fun on the other side of that. You've been waiting a long time to test those defenses, haven't you? Impressive work as always. I see you've developed a thing for vines."

She hadn't quite realized she'd worried about his reaction, but there was no judgment, just appreciation for her skill. What a novel experience.

Theira's lips quirked. "Thank you. I did experiment with some new vine spells, and it's always nice to see them in action. Would you set these on the table please? I'll figure out what to do with them later."

She opened her hands to reveal the broken shards of the mug.

His grin fell, and his gaze pierced her. "Of course," he said as he opened his hands to her, voice gruff in a way that made her chest tighten.

It was *pottery*, for Gaia's sake.

Varius accepted the shards, and her hands brushed his. No reason for that slight touch to send a zing of awareness through her.

She glanced up at him again, finding his gaze intent.

"Are you not finished outside?" he rumbled.

Theira sighed, stepping back and removing her cloak. "No. I doubt anyone will be back soon, but I'll need to ready the ground in case. Remove the bodies, make sure I'm not poisoning anything I don't mean to, reinvigorate the exhausted spells. You know."

"Ah." Varius opened his mouth to say something then thought better of it, considering her. "I'll stay out of your way then."

The best she could hope for. It wasn't as though he could assist, even if he wanted to, which he would know. Theira inclined her head in thanks and headed back out to the garden.

This was a different kind of work. Letting loose was fun, but adjusting spells required a distinct mindset. Taking stock of power levels, pruning as needed, clearing the ground. Careful attention to detail and precise applications of sorcery—satisfying but grueling.

It was also more exhausting to expend power this way without the rush of battle, if familiar deep in her bones. She supplemented the spells with her power, draining it little by little.

Theira had other, untouched spells inside the house if either her garden's exhaustion or hers became an issue, but she didn't think Varius had any nefarious intentions toward her—not that he was incapable of deception, but he was, at his heart, an honest man. If he were planning to attack her, she'd know. She wouldn't lower her defenses for anything less—possibly anyone else.

The fact that a man of his character didn't believe she was worth killing after everything she'd done might have been humbling, if she were the type for humility. Instead she was... not quite hopeful. Touched, perhaps.

Even with her immediate ministrations, the garden wouldn't recover all at once. She didn't carry enough power for that within her, and she'd avoid draining her jewel reserves unless they did in fact receive more visitors sooner than she expected.

But she did as much as she could to speed the recovery and then looked up at the sun. Bursts of sorcery could be very impressive, but this kind of long, painstaking work was what separated the flashy from the survivors under Castle Korossia. The aftermath of the minutes-long battle had taken her hours, and only now that she was done did she allow herself to notice how tired she was.

Theira sighed as she stretched, and then began to trudge back toward the house. She should have waited a little longer to notice that, until she'd had time to eat something. Maybe she was out of practice after all, but not so much that she couldn't grit her teeth and muster enough energy to cook. She'd feel worse if she collapsed without food. Potions could help in an emergency, but this wasn't one.

She might yet have an actual emergency, after all.

Theira restrained a groan at the effort to haul open her impressive but heavy door, kicking her boots off in the empty entryway. No Varius to greet her this time, and she was annoyed at the prick of disappointment she felt.

What did she expect, he would stand in the entryway and wait for her like a dog? That having welcomed her home after a battle once, he'd be there for her every time? Just because he was rock-solid didn't mean she should depend on him.

Theira scowled at herself as she made her way to the kitchen, trying to summon anger rather than obscure disappointment. She wouldn't be sad about her life—impossibly free, despite every odd!—if she could stop hoping for unreasonable things.

And then she saw Varius standing in her kitchen.

"Oh good, you're back." He turned and smiled at her.

Theira's heart stopped.

The most dangerous general she'd ever faced was standing in her kitchen, stirring a pot, wearing an apron. *Her* apron.

It was absolutely unfair for him to look so sexy wearing an apron.

She knew it was the incongruity. She did. It still took an effort of will to summon her jaw back up from the floor

"I hope you don't mind, I let myself into your pantry," Varius said casually, turning back away from her like there was nothing remotely remarkable about this situation. Was this how he'd felt when she made him tea? "It looked like everything was organized to avoid poisoning by accident, but you may want to make sure. I'm not experiencing any numbness or trouble breathing though."

He would know the signs of her usual efforts in that direction, Theira thought with surreal detachment.

As he carried out a tray with a bowl of hot soup and half a loaf of bread.

"You must be starving after all that," Varius said. "Sit down and eat. I'll join you in a minute."

Theira stared at him.

He stared back.

Then he smiled, joy spilling into his eyes, and as her heart jolted back to life Varius set the tray on the table, returned behind her, and took her by the shoulders.

She snapped to attention.

He gently pushed her into a chair.

Theira technically *could* melt into the floor, and she gave the notion some serious consideration.

But then she'd only have to face him later with *more* embarrassment and less food.

"No accidental poison?" Varius prompted.

Theira checked, shook her head.

He let out a breath. "Good. Some welcome home that would be, if I spent all morning wasting your defenses on inedible soup. I'll be right back."

He vanished back to the kitchen, and Theira shoved a bite of soup in her mouth in hopes it would prevent her from turning to stare at him.

It didn't.

Varius was cleaning up after himself, and she tracked him as he crossed to the entryway with a towel and one of her cleaning potions. How had he identified it? Had he tested every likely bottle until he found one that suited his need?

Goddess, probably. He was smart and thorough, and after surviving years of her tricks he knew her better than anyone.

Theira heard two soft thumps from the entryway, and belatedly she realized what he was doing.

Moving her muddy boots to the tray. Cleaning up after *her*.

Not letting the war follow her back into her home.

Theira wrenched her focus back to the table, fighting inexplicable tears.

Varius hadn't met her at the door a second time, but only because he'd been making her lunch. He *could* make her lunch, and she could eat it without fear. He knew her well enough to know what she'd need, even when she hadn't asked for it. And she'd thought he'd decided he couldn't help her? She should have known *him* better than that.

She'd missed the welcome, but the feeling of finding him working in her kitchen on her behalf—she didn't have words for this.

Varius set his tray down across from her. "Can I make you some tea?"

"No, thank you. I'll get some myself in a bit."

Varius narrowed his eyes, and Theira absurdly found herself flushing. The response had been reflexive, but it also *would* be more expedient for her to brew something herself than to try to explain to him how to make it properly.

She was suddenly getting the sense that he wouldn't accept that answer for long.

If he were here for a long time, anyway.

"The soup is perfect," she said instead, softer than she'd intended. "Thank you."

"You are welcome," Varius rumbled.

Theira suppressed a shiver. At his voice, and at the suspicion that he meant that literally.

She was welcome. With him. What was she supposed to do with that?

Her eyes snagged on his tray, and her breath caught.

Varius had reassembled the shattered mug—mostly.

He followed her gaze. "I thought I'd take stock of what we could do with this. It's missing a big piece, though."

We.

She was a First-Tier Adept Sorceress, the only one alive who'd eluded the best efforts of both Korossia and the Aurelian Empire, she was the Sorceress bloody Transcendent, and she would *not* cry.

"It's embedded in Kryseia's heart," Theira explained.

"Ah." He nodded, like this was a normal thing to say to someone, and she supposed for them it was. "Well, normal glue probably wouldn't have worked anyway. We'll have to figure out something else. Do you have sorcerous glue?"

"I could make some." Not something she'd ever considered.

Something new, she could use her skill for. Not instead of, but in addition to destruction.

A project she didn't have to do alone.

"There was a pottery book in my room. I'll take a look at that later, unless you have another idea?"

Beyond words, Theira mutely shook her head.

Varius nodded, like they'd decided on a plan of action. Theira's head spun, but it was possible that was just due to dehydration so she ate some more soup in case that would help.

"So," he said, and Theira breathed a sigh of relief—he was ready to talk business, a thing she knew how to do.

But he heard her exhale and paused, trying to work out what it meant.

Varius apparently, thankfully, decided not to press, though, because he continued, "What problems will this cause for you? Tychon didn't interfere when you left before, even if he didn't like it, but now that you've stood against him I can't see him letting that go."

Theira nodded, ripping off a chunk of bread to dip in the soup. "He won't. But he's also not so arrogant that he'll come after me here, where I've had years to control the ground. Certainly not now that I've proved I'm ready."

"Don't take this the wrong way," Varius said, "but is he not powerful enough to take you on head-to-head, even here? I thought that was the whole reason no one rebelled against him."

"Oh, he is," Theira said without offense. "The Sorcerer Ascendant can draw on enough power to defeat anyone in a head-to-head battle. He just wouldn't come through unscathed, and I could drain him enough that another sorceress would finish the job. Which I would, and they would, and he knows that. That's why you never see him on the battlefield."

"Ah. I'd always thought it was an aversion to doing his own work when he could force it on others and cull his competition."

"It's that as well, of course. But Korossia needs ever more resources to support the level of sorcery and luxury those at the top have become accustomed to—that is, ostensibly, the whole reason Korossia is in this war. But if there are fewer high-tier sorcerers to sustain, more of those resources go to Tychon."

"Making him more powerful with every year that passes without lifting a finger. Elegant."

"Quite."

Varius grunted, leaning back in his seat and ripping off a piece of bread for himself. He might be fully dressed today, but even the man's forearms were unreasonable, their strength so visibly evident even at rest, unlike her own. "Not so different from the empire, really, although there are a few more hands at the head to split the rewards. They can't justify the taxes that keep them in luxury without war, and a holy war against evil sorcery unites all the disparate nations so they don't rebel against the wealthy few."

"A tale as old as time."

He sighed. "It's no wonder neither side will end this disaster. The ones with all the power are too invested to stop without taking a hit themselves, which they'll never do."

Varius frowned down at the remains of his soup—how had he eaten that so fast? Soldier habits, she supposed—which Theira took heart from. He was brooding on the problem now, and that was a big step up from only yesterday, even if she wasn't sure what had changed for him besides some rest.

Then he said, "So if you ever leave your territory here, Tychon will send sorceresses to hunt you."

Ah. Not brooding, planning. Ever the strategist.

"Yes. But I'm in no rush to go anywhere."

She'd traveled plenty during the war. Seen sights, burned them. Theira was happy to stay in this place she'd carved for herself.

Now, anyway. Later—

"I don't like you being trapped here, though," Varius said. He ripped his bread precisely, a fraction of the force she knew he could exert.

It thrilled her, his control.

And made her want to break it.

Perhaps later, once she had enough energy to do something about an unleashed Varius, though she was feeling more energized every minute in his presence. Their banter across battlefields—as she surprised him with a new kind of sorcerous trap and got to deliver a prepared quip that had him rolling his eyes in amusement even as he struggled to free all his soldiers, or he surprised her by neatly avoiding it and teasing her mercilessly for underestimating him as she was forced to rapidly improvise new defenses—had always been something she unreasonably looked forward to; she might have expected what he would do to her in closer quarters.

"There's no way for sorcerers to surround me," she assured him.

"I meant you should be free to go where you choose." Before Theira had to think of a response to that breathtaking statement, from a former enemy of all people, he continued, "If Caius Sobanus and his ilk were really clever they'd have reached out to you about joining forces once you'd gotten away to end this. But there's too much bigotry in the empire for them to have even considered it."

"Be fair, I have also killed quite a lot of your people," Theira said, amused, but then let her smile fall to meet his gaze seriously. "And I don't want the Aurelian Empire to win the war, either. I want *both of them* to stop their aggression. The nightmare needs to end for everyone."

An impossibly bold idea. People on both sides had been executed for suggesting less.

Varius just raised his eyebrows. "Do you really think that's possible?"

He couldn't even imagine it.

But he was asking. Theira returned, "Do you believe your people deserve to rest?"

"Yes," Varius said without hesitation. "And so do you."

She had her freedom. But as his steady gaze held hers, Theira realized that for Varius, it wasn't enough. He wanted more—for *her*.

Her chest tightened again as she leaned forward across the table. "Then so do *you*."

Varius made a face. "You know, I felt that coming and still walked into it."

Theira laughed, easing back in her seat and popping another soup-soaked piece of bread into her mouth. A bit of soup leaked out, and as she grabbed a cloth to wipe it she noticed Varius tracking her lips.

An excellent sign, if she did say so herself.

So Theira pressed a little. "If you can't imagine freedom for yourself, how can you expect anyone else to hope enough for themselves to do anything about it?"

He studied her. "How did you do it? How did you even imagine you could leave?"

Theira thought. "I suppose I didn't, at first. But I started making plans in case. To give me something else to think about besides the war. To see if I could get away with it. And little by little I'd invested enough resources and time in my little side project that I started to believe in it in truth. So when the time came and I knew I had to get out or die in this war, it—it was still a shift. But not an earth-shattering one all at once. Your path will necessarily be different."

"Because I didn't try."

"Because I had time to adjust, and you didn't."

Varius shook his head. "Even after you left, I didn't quite believe it. And then I thought, of course Theira would be the one person able to find a way to escape this nightmare, and that still wasn't enough of a kick in the pants to get me thinking."

"Now *that* I don't believe," Theira said firmly. "You thought about it. You just didn't see a way out that wouldn't abandon or hurt your people."

Varius pursed his lips but didn't debate the point.

Theira huffed. *So* honest, even when he didn't like the answers. That was one of the things that had always made him difficult—he saw too much.

And he proved it as he said, "Whereas you didn't have anyone who depended on your presence, but you hoped they might depend on your absence. What were you going to do, if a house's worth of sorceresses followed you?"

"The table extends to seat more. I have extra chairs."

It slipped out. It wasn't what she'd have said if she'd taken a second to think about it, and she knew that wasn't what he was asking, not really.

But maybe it was, because Varius said softly, "The whole house is like that, isn't it? Ready and adaptable in case anyone else ever dared believe. And you don't just have the craft books because you needed to be able to be self-sufficient."

He did always see too much.

Theira looked around her house that still felt, despite her best efforts, like it was missing something.

And maybe that something was people.

"I wanted them to be able to find something else they could do purely for the joy of it, if they wanted. That's not a part of our upbringing, sorceresses." Oh, that would sound pathetic to him, wouldn't it? She flashed him a grin in a pitiful attempt to cover. "If you want to take up pottery, I'm prepared to make that happen."

"And you?" Varius asked, gaze inexorable, refusing to be distracted. "Did you try something?"

Theira hesitated. Would he laugh? Of course he wouldn't laugh. Unless maybe she laughed, and they could laugh about it together? She wasn't sure what response she even wanted, so she evaded. "I tried a few things."

"What did you settle on?"

Inexorable. He wouldn't believe she'd just given up the effort. Theira shrugged self-consciously and decided to just come out with it. "Painting. I can be as messy as I want and still make something, even if it isn't beautiful. My standards are low."

"No, they aren't," Varius said with a thread of amusement, "but it's not something it matters to be good at. Just that you have the freedom to do."

Yes. That was it exactly.

She tried to make a joke of it. "Some of us need to practice being imperfect."

He snorted. "You refused to continue with something you were naturally better at, didn't you?"

Well. Maybe.

Theira glanced down at her tray for a distraction, but she'd tragically finished all the food already. Curses.

Then he asked, "Will you show me?"

Theira froze. Her eyes darted up to his.

Varius' gaze was steady. "Your art. The house. All of it."

Did she want that? Yes and no.

She wanted to show someone, and him in particular, so desperately she was terrified to.

And that, ultimately, was what decided her.

Not that she could trust him, though she thought she could. But the Sorceress Transcendent didn't cower for anyone, and certainly not herself.

Varius knew what she would answer. He stood and held out a hand.

Not because she needed it. But because he could offer.

She clasped onto him, and let him help her to her feet.

Varius was very careful as Theira gave him a tour of her home. Too effusive, and she'd think he was mocking her; too silent, and she'd shrivel inside and never let on except for a slow withdrawal from their relationship, whatever it was. That was the last thing he wanted.

He wanted her to feel free, and even though she'd escaped physically, she clearly didn't. The past *hadn't* followed her here, but for Theira, that was a problem. She'd never rest easy until she had resolution, too.

Varius couldn't help with that, though in a way, perhaps his arrival was a kind of boon in that regard—she'd have to deal with it now. Whether there was a way to move on, he didn't know.

But he could look with unfeigned interest as Theira showed him the space she'd made for herself, and ask intelligent questions, and let her experience, for the first time, finally, what it might be like to share her home with another person.

His chest ached at the thought. Unconscionable, that she'd never had this before. Poignant, that he was her first.

And *that* was a thought to rein in, because interested she might be but accepting of his possessive urges was something beyond.

Theira had grown more relaxed as they proceeded through the house—the many guest rooms, a sitting room with haphazard books and a view of her garden, a peek into a precisely ordered laboratory that apparently had better protections against sorcerous surprises than the kitchen—but there was one room she hesitated at.

"You don't have to show me your bedroom," Varius said.

Theira shook her head, which didn't surprise him—that would probably be the door at the end of the hall. "It's not that."

Then she opened it, and here was where he felt her presence like the kitchen.

Which was to say, it was a disaster.

Color everywhere in various textures, made with different tools and mixes, sheets discarded, mounted across walls, fabrics in baskets, a shelf of pottery.

Varius smiled. "Your art room. I love it."

Theira looked at him and seemed to decide he was serious. She shrugged. "It's a bit of a mess."

"I'm shocked."

"What's that supposed to mean?"

Varius lifted his chin in the direction of most of the canvases. "You decided on painting in a freeform style, didn't you? Your sorcery is always so precise—so that would be a departure. Something new."

Theira's lips curved. "I should have asked you to recommend me an artform. My sorcerous skills still come in handy for the composition of the paints."

He shook his head. "Better to explore. May I look?"

She gestured forward without a word, and he carefully stepped inside.

"You won't track paint outside the room," she told him.

Varius grinned. "You think of everything, my transcendence."

Theira snorted but relaxed a little further. He looked more closely at the paintings he could see, smiling—all bold colors, wild and raw. Some were clearly experiments with textures or techniques, but others—

Varius' breath caught as he gazed at one, the warm, bright, expansive blend of colors. "This is the hill above the Tridentis. Before the battle. You were there?"

"How in Gaia's name can you tell that?"

"The cast of light between the sky and the river at dawn—I recognize that reflection. You've evoked it beautifully here."

Theira was studying him like a puzzle. "You can really tell that just by looking at my mishmash of paint."

"Your art," Varius said gently. "I know you, Theira. And I am used to looking for you in chaos."

A quick grin. "And finding me."

His chest warmed. "Just in time for whatever you've made this time. I am surprised you've seen the hill from that direction."

Theira rocked her head noncommittally. "I've laid a lot of spells over the years."

Evasive—what did she have to hide from him now? Or maybe she just wanted him to figure it—her—out.

He would.

He always did.

And it hadn't been for purely practical reasons for a long time.

"Is there room in here for a second person?" Varius asked.

"You want to try painting?"

Next to her fearless expression? No. And he didn't want that to become a competition between them.

"Maybe something else," he mused. "It's been a long time since I've had the chance to build something rather than break it. Do you have any clay in your garden?" He thought he knew which book could teach him how to fix her broken mug.

Theira was studying him again—he had the impression that she was sizing him up, but for what?

Varius shook his head. "That was presumptuous, wasn't it? I probably won't have time—"

"You will," Theira interrupted firmly. "You *will* have time. And I have all kinds of materials you can play with on the lower level. Let's see what we can find that looks interesting to you."

Varius looked up. "There's an underground?"

Theira smiled. "I'm a sorceress, Varius. Of course there's a hidden level underground."

Varius had been wrong—the door at the end of the hallway was not to Theira's bedroom, but to a staircase that led underneath her house.

He mentally calculated as they descended. Given how far they were going, she had a fucking hippodrome buried under the hill.

"Did you want to make sure Tychon couldn't come at you from belowground?" he asked her.

"That's one reason," Theira agreed. "But it's also heavily spelled. *Really* heavily spelled. Sometimes you want to try something especially destructive and don't want to destroy the garden, you know?"

Varius snorted. "I do know," he agreed dryly.

Gods, the times he would have given for an empty field for military exercises.

They reached the bottom at last. Theira opened a door, snapped her fingers, and light flooded the space.

It *was* the size of an arena.

Theira immediately started walking one way, but Varius had frozen at what was on the other side.

He suddenly struggled to breathe.

"Theira," he croaked.

"Yes?"

Varius took a deep breath, unable to tear his eyes away. "What am I looking at?"

"Hmm? Oh, that," she said offhandedly.

"'Oh, that'?" he echoed incredulously. "What bullshit. You brought me down to notice this, didn't you? The hell am I looking at?"

Theira's wild hair swirled around her as she slowly stepped back toward him, gauging his response.

"I did wonder what you'd make of it." She finally looked away from him and toward the object of their discussion. "What do you think it is?"

"It looks," Varius said, his voice tight, "like an army."

And not just any army.

In the cavernous space under her home, Theira was storing what looked like hundreds of giant figures made of stone—no, clay.

Varius laughed roughly. Did she have clay in her garden. She'd built a godscursed army out of it.

They were human-like—upright, two legs and arms, a head—but proportioned differently. The head was more like a dome, the limbs enormous. If they could move, a swing from one of those fists would crush a man. It would crush a *dozen* men.

And there were hundreds.

"They're called golems," Theira said. "I started building them after I moved here, in anticipation."

Of the war coming to her door.

She'd left the war behind, but she'd never believed she was free of it.

She played in her kitchen and made art and built space for refugees and also an entire inanimate army.

"So they *do* move?" Varius asked.

"Oh yes. Here, I'll show you." Theira narrowed her eyes and waved a hand.

Two glowing red dots appeared in the 'head' of one of the golems.

Then another.

Varius glanced at Theira, her brow furrowed in concentration, then back at the golems in awe.

The two golems took a huge step together in tandem. Then another, and another.

Varius imagined a hundred of these coming at him on a battlefield, visions of death and destruction flashing through his mind.

One of the golems raised an arm as if to swing, and Varius held his breath.

Then all of a sudden their eyes winked out and they went still.

Theira puffed out a breath and muttered something he didn't catch but was probably profane.

"And that's the problem," she grumbled. "They're immune to practically any degree of sorcery, and I can animate them all at the same time. I have a... well, to simplify, a sorcerous array that links them all together and allows me to activate them with barely any of my own power.

"But I can't control them separately. I can march them all in a line, and they can all swing at the same time, but making them do two different tasks? Well, I can usually manage two, though I stopped practicing. But three? A dozen? No." She puffed out another breath. "It's frustrating. It was such a *good* idea."

"It's an *incredible* idea," Varius told her. His mind spun.

This was why she needed a house away from Tychon's watch. It was all for this.

Theira sighed. "But with that limitation, their usage in a real engagement is too limited. If they marched on a town, I wouldn't be able to keep them from walking through houses, because I couldn't change their directions. If they faced different kinds of attacks?" She shook her head. "I've resorted to using them as test dummies. Though as a person who's actually led an army and routinely had to counter all manner of unexpected circumstances, I admit I hoped you might be able to come up with a more useful idea for them. I've been loath to abandon the concept entirely, but—"

"I have *so many* ideas," Varius interrupted. "The first is: this array. Is there a way *I* can try controlling them?"

Theira blinked. Cocked her head. "Hmm. Yes, I think so. Why?"

"Your strength is in advance planning," Varius told her. "*My* job is to keep track of a thousand things at once while they're changing and adapt."

Theira's eyes lit. "What an interesting point. Come this way."

She strode quickly into the sea of golems, and Varius followed the sorceress deeper in, wondering what he was getting into and excited about it.

He really hadn't been a proper Aurelian soldier.

Theira stopped at one golem that had a step stool next to it and gestured him up. "This golem's head opens. You can control it from inside. I'd thought it might be advantageous to be armored, though I couldn't stand it. There's an... I don't know how to explain it. Drop yourself in, have a look around. I'll get you set up from outside."

Varius had been the top enemy of sorceresses for years. He didn't understand this magic, and it would be impossibly easy for her to have set something up where he stepped into her spell and she controlled his body.

The fact that Theira had distractedly scurried away without even waiting to see what he would do was the best reassurance on offer.

But really—Varius wasn't any better than her. He'd joked she wouldn't have been able to resist opening her door to him, and he was absolutely going to get in her clay death puppet.

He jumped into the golem.

"Pull the top closed!" Theira called.

Sealing him inside her sorcerous death puppet?

Varius sighed and gripped the lever above his head.

If she didn't take this as a show of trust from him, he wasn't sure what would do it.

As soon as the head shut, it was like windows had opened all around him.

Varius reached forward through the vision and touched solid clay. But he could see all the golems surrounding him as if there were no barrier.

"Can you hear me?" Theira's voice abruptly appeared as if next to his ear.

What the fuck? "Yes."

"Fantastic. I'm going to connect you to just this golem first, so you can try moving it. Ready?"

How in all the gods' names could he possibly be ready for this madness?

Varius grinned. "Yes."

He had no idea what Theira did—*sorcery*—but all at once he felt a kind of disassociation with his body. There were no words to describe it—he could hardly think in words, like he'd descended all at once into a strange drug haze—but he could *feel* the golem in his mind.

And he could move it.

Varius didn't take a step with his body. He took a step with his brain.

And then another.

"Perfect! Ready for another?"

He'd never heard her sound so excited. It took Varius a second to find his speech again. "Yes."

There was no possible other answer. Not now.

Theira added another golem, and another, and Varius adjusted.

He tried different movements, testing their range of motion, their speed, their strength. A controlled punch was difficult because they didn't coil or spring well, but a swing of the arm would be deadly. He felt resistance when he hit another golem as strong as the first, but no reverberating pain. And after a quick adjustment from Theira, the cursed things could jump—Varius could level a house in one move like that, smashing through the roof.

Once he had the hang of controlling them separately, he told Theira, "Give me all of them."

A beat. "Are you sure?"

Was she hesitating, now that she'd granted him access to this terrifying power? No, she could disconnect him at any time—this was worry for him. "I need to know what I'm working with."

She took him at his word. "One full golem army, here you go."

And then it was like Varius' brain exploded.

He didn't know what his real eyes were seeing. He could see at the same time everything the golems could see—all of them at once. And he was aware, suddenly, of all the different bodies around him, like they were extensions of himself.

What would it be like, to command an army like this?

Could his mind truly handle this?

Varius took a breath.

With the whole golem army, he took one single step.

Boom. The sound resounded through the underground.

Then another.

His head felt like it was splitting from the pressure. *Just one more step.*

Just one more.

Just one more—

Varius' eyes snapped wide.

"Varius?" Theira's voice, almost distant. "Are you still with me?"

In answer, Varius took another step.

Then a separate golem took a step at a different time.

And another.

Slowly, breathing deeply, Varius moved hundreds of monstrous clay warriors with his mind as if running an army maneuver, like the most precise of his soldiers in tandem.

Inexorably, they surrounded where Theira stood tall in the center of the arena, her hair floating wildly around her. He arrayed the solid clay forms he controlled around her.

And then every golem but his bent down on one knee, while Varius' extended a hand.

"I'm with you," he said. "Let's see what we can do together."

Theira's expression turned fierce and exultant, and as sweat streamed off him, Varius felt it too.

All at once, they had a chance.

Together.

Chapter 4

Days passed, and they practiced.

Or perhaps more accurately, they played.

Theira stood in the back of her underground, watching as Varius' golem army tore through the shield-wall of opponents she'd animated for him. Her side didn't do anything but stand and punch on repeat, a pattern she could activate and then leave off controlling.

They were a delaying tactic for the real setup.

As one of his golems breached the line, it set off one of her spells, which detonated, sending a spray of rock and dirt into the air.

The sorcery-resistant golem was unaffected, but Varius' vision wasn't.

He'd learned to arrange formations around one golem—not the one he was inside—to give himself a point of focus, a way to help him filter and process the information. And now, when that golem ran into difficulty, he rapidly chose a golem in another position and switched.

They could only practice for so long before he was too mentally exhausted to continue, but it took longer every day, and they were able to get more and more sessions in.

Theira, frankly, was still astonished not even just that Varius could control all the golems, but at his level of sophistication.

One of his golems hurled one of hers across the room—which required Varius to manipulate clay arms and use them in a way unlike a human's—at the same moment another kicked debris out of the way and yet another advanced.

He didn't make each of them do complex motions simultaneously, but instead batched them, with either multiple teams of golems collectively doing the same maneuver or different sections of his army executing particular tasks.

And while Varius exulted in personally controlling an invincible army that would do whatever he wanted exactly to his own limits and he never had to worry about their injuries or death, Theira got to play.

No risk of hurting Varius, let alone the golems or her house.

So she unleashed explosions to blot Varius' vision, or triggered illusions to turn the hall black as night, or launched bombs that filled the room with acidic haze.

She caught golems in traps of vines or her new sticky glue, while others arrested mid-step to change direction.

She drowned one in a pool of hot clay only to realize she'd melted the golem, so that wasn't one to repeat except for extraordinary circumstances.

They had always been each other's best match.

Sometimes Theira won, or Varius tired before they could finish. Some days his sorcery-invincible golems plowed through all her improvisations, or her newest experiments failed spectacularly.

But no matter the outcome, every time ended with Theira's blood singing.

She thought Varius loved it too, but though she'd catch heat in his gaze and he'd flirt, he hadn't made a move toward anything more.

Now that he'd finally seen a way to end the war, she guessed he was imagining the life he could go back to in the Aurelian Empire. Varius was an all-or-nothing sort, so she should be glad he cared enough not to start something he didn't intend to finish.

So Theira would be his friend, and his accomplice, and if together they could end a war and then perhaps meet occasionally for dinner, she could live with that. It wasn't what she wanted, but it was more than she'd had before, and she would survive.

But her heart still raced when Varius climbed golems on top of golems, balancing them to make a tower to reach the sorcerous construct she'd been using to spray sticky goo all over the field as well as covering their 'eyes', and pulled it from the air.

Theira was already launching her next attack and had to quickly deactivate it when Varius popped open his golem's top and lifted himself out.

Shirtless, as he always practiced, and she could not decide whether he was taunting her on purpose.

"That's it for me right now," he said.

Shorter than she'd expected, but he'd tried several new things; that probably wore on him. She couldn't be too disappointed when she was having more fun now than she'd had... perhaps ever.

"Your control of their movements is even better than yesterday," Theira said as he landed and walked toward her. "I'm amazed you can direct them all to make minute adjustments while the rest of your army still accomplishes multiple tasks."

"It's the balance that's the tricky part," Varius agreed. "The golems aren't all the same shape on the outside, which I don't really feel through my awareness. I have to adapt."

Hmm. Maybe she could use that next time.

Varius grinned at her. "Yes, make me practice. I don't want you to get too bored with all the same things. I'm amazed how quickly you can come up with new ideas."

"I've always had plenty of ideas," Theira said. "Testing was the limiting factor."

He laughed, running a hand through his curls. "Well, I'm glad to assist you with some real-time feedback."

It *was* useful. Theira judged her success rate by how quickly Varius could counter her, and in what way. If he relied on invincibility, she had a winner. If a spell worked on him once, another general would struggle with it. If he countered immediately, it wasn't worth investing time into, even if it was only because he knew her well.

If she went back to war, it would only be once.

"I want to show you something," Varius said.

Theira raised her eyebrows and gestured for him to hop back in the golem.

"Upstairs," he amended. Even more curious. "Let's get something to eat."

He kept doing that. Knocking on the door to her lab and bringing her water when she'd been focused on her experiments for too long. Cleaning up dishes after she cooked. Asking her if he could wash her blankets while he was doing his.

Every time, it startled her, and made her feel... soft, perhaps. She shouldn't get used to it. He'd make some Aurelian woman a fantastic husband, and she tried not to resent that but didn't succeed.

Theira followed him to the kitchen, but he stopped before they got there. She raised her eyebrows again, and Varius shifted on his feet and took a breath.

He was nervous?

He angled toward the wall and Theira followed his gaze, only then noticing what he wanted to show her, so intent she'd been on watching the line of his back.

Her breath caught.

Her painting of the sky above the Tridentis was mounted on the wall, and she recognized the wooden frame. Varius had been busy cutting, sanding, carving, and staining bits of wood for days.

Right in front of her, and she hadn't understood.

"I loved this painting first." Varius' voice was rough. "It's so full of color and life, and I can practically feel your wonder looking up into the sky. And selfishly, it's a place where our paths didn't quite cross, but were still entwined. My world, with you always moving through it."

Theira couldn't say anything around the lump in her throat.

Varius swallowed. "You deserve for your home to be beautiful, Theira. And for it to be your home, your mark should be all the way through it. Even if you think it's messy. I know my frame here isn't perfect either—"

"It is."

Varius stepped forward and took her unresisting hand. "Exactly. We made this. *We made this.* It would be beautiful anyway, but it's also beautiful *because* of that, and every time I see it you remind me to dream bigger. So I put it on the wall, and I hope, in the future, I can keep covering this house with more of us. If you want."

In the future.

Keep.

Oh, she'd been wrong. He wasn't saving himself at all.

The general was biding his time until he had the perfect play.

And he had *absolutely* been torturing her on purpose.

Theira's hand tightened on his, and she took a step closer to him too.

All the way closer, pressing her body flush against his naked, sweaty muscles.

Turnabout, enemy mine.

Varius' pupils darkened.

Theira put her other hand against his chest, feeling his racing heart. And he let her.

But he also wrapped *his* other arm around her back, holding her close. Holding her *there*, with him.

Theira tilted her head and whispered into his ear as he shuddered, her blood singing for an entirely different reason. "You didn't call a halt because you were tired, did you."

His thumb stroked hers in small circles and his other hand mimicked it on her back.

As he stroked down, and down.

Maybe her blood sang for the same reason.

"I wanted to be sure," Varius murmured, "I had enough energy for whatever you might have in mind. I'm all warmed up for you."

Gaia, so was she.

Varius' voice was a low, delicious rumble as he asked, "Are you hungry, Theira?"

In answer, Theira snaked the hand on his chest up around his neck and pulled him down for a kiss.

His lips met hers, then his tongue, the kiss as fierce as she felt and growing ever hotter.

Theira wrapped her legs around him, and with his ridiculous muscles he supported her effortlessly—and then he turned and pushed her into the wall, right underneath their framed painting.

Theira grinned against his lips and pushed his face back, just for a moment, so she could watch his reaction.

As she levitated them both.

"Ever had magical sex, Varius?" Theira purred. "Because you're about to."

The unbridled delight in his gaze—for *her*—was everything. "Only in my dreams," he said. "I'd be happy to show you what I've imagined."

"Let's see what we can do together," Theira said.

She teleported them to her bedroom, and let the world vanish for a little while.

As Varius stirred the paint for a new frame, he watched Theira across the art room. Usually her movements were smooth and deliberate, but here, she played. She flicked the brush, she zig-zagged it quickly. She studied what she'd done and switched to the reverse end of her brush to scrape a line through the paint, just to see what it would do.

Varius smiled to see it. She could do whatever struck her, and she did, without fear or self-consciousness. Even knowing he was in the same room and could see her.

She let him see all of her.

"I can feel you watching me," Theira remarked, but she didn't stop painting.

The old instincts were still with them.

"I like watching you," Varius replied just as easily.

Theira glanced over her shoulder with a smirk. "I know."

Memories of watching her naked body above him that morning flashed through his mind, and Varius' blood rushed to the predictable area.

Given the amount of sex they'd been having the last few days, he'd thought his desire might have started to calm by now—he wasn't exactly a young man anymore, though Theira assured him she could produce an effective potion for any situation if needed—but if anything it was increasing. Like regular exposure was teaching his body it could have as much as he could handle.

And both of them, it turned out, could handle quite a lot.

In the last few days, they'd shifted into a new pattern. They made love in Theira's room, and Varius stayed there while they slept. A profound level of unspoken trust from both of them.

And it was also more than that. They trained in the underground twice every day. But they also made art together, and cooked and cleaned in the same room, and now even spent time reading quietly, still together. Like they couldn't quite bear to not be in physical proximity if they didn't have to.

It was a degree of bone-deep comfort Varius had never experienced with anyone, and he was like a starving man inhaling the bounty before him unable to stop, like he couldn't quite believe he wouldn't be starving again soon. He craved her with every part of him, and he'd experienced enough sorcery to know this wasn't any kind of magic Theira had worked on purpose. When she spent time tending her garden or working in her lab, his whole being ached at the loss.

But she was here now.

And he was still hungry.

Varius set his painting aside and approached Theira slowly, loving that she knew he was coming—he could see the smile curving on her cheek—but didn't tense. Just waited in a spirit of mischief to see what he would do.

He wrapped his arms around her middle and bent to kiss her ear, her cheek. Down her neck. She tilted her head to give him better access, her pulse accelerating, though she didn't stop painting.

That was the game then. To see how far he could go before she was irrevocably distracted.

Varius' own smile stretched as he nipped her lightly, reveling in the catch of her breath.

Then all at once Theira's head snapped up, and only his battle-honed reaction time saved him from a broken nose.

Theira was tense now, and not in a fun way. Her head swiveled in the direction of a paint-spattered wall, but her eyes were unfocused.

She was looking farther than he could see.

That was the direction of the Aurelian Empire.

Varius' arms tightened around her. "What is it?"

"One of my spells in the empire tripped," Theira said tightly. "People are crossing a boundary in large numbers, and it's not the border between our countries—it's *away* from the border."

Varius frowned. The Aurelian Empire wouldn't cede that border for anything.

Then all at once it made sense.

"Aurelian citizens are fleeing," he said grimly, "*from the empire.*"

Even his departure hadn't been enough for Sobanus to abandon his plan of slaughtering their own citizens. Or maybe this was part of a ploy to draw him out.

It would work.

Theira set down her paintbrush and turned in his arms.

Varius' stomach dropped. He closed his eyes and bowed his head. This wasn't how he wanted this.

They'd been preparing to stop a war. Not a specific plan, not yet, but they now unilaterally had enough leverage to make either side shut up and pay attention.

And if they were going to use that to make a difference, the time was upon them now.

Theira's gentle hand on his cheek made him look at her, and he gazed directly into the deep, wild pools of her eyes.

"I wanted more time," Varius whispered.

To prepare, yes. But he meant *with her.*

No amount of preparation would change that they were planning to attempt the impossible. And that meant the chance of failure was high.

"I know," Theira agreed softly.

Varius crushed his mouth to hers, and she met him in kind. This kiss was, in its way, as fierce as their first, but this time it was tinged with desperation. Longing, even though she was still right in front of him.

Love, at least from him.

And whatever she felt for him, for this, he didn't want to rush, to behave as if they had to say everything that mattered as soon as possible. He wanted them to have all the time in the world to feel whatever they felt, to explore this beautiful, unlikely thing they'd found together.

When they finally broke for air, Varius lowered his forehead to hers and breathed deeply. "We'll have more," he swore to her.

This was his favorite smile of hers: a little soft.

And all wicked.

His heart soared.

"Good," Theira said. "I do so hate to lay plans that I never get to employ. Let's go stop a war, shall we?"

Plans for him, or plans for battle?

Varius resolved they'd both live long enough for him to find out.

And if it wasn't the former, he'd just have to work a little harder to convince her he was worth keeping around.

But first, the fastest way to a sorceress' heart was slaughtering the enemies she didn't care to deal with herself.

"Do you have a plan?" he asked. Teased, almost.

Theira smiled, one he hadn't seen in a long time. Fierce, yes. But a little wild.

And maybe a little nervous.

That was new.

"Trust me," the Sorceress Transcendent said, "to handle my side."

Varius' heart lurched. Even now that they were on the same side, she wasn't going to share this with him? Hiding from him still?

He searched her gaze. And took a breath.

He did trust her. So if she wasn't telling him everything, there was a reason.

"Then I'll handle mine," Varius said, and couldn't quite parse the emotion that flickered through her eyes—relief, but something else, too. "Let's go."

CHAPTER 5

Theira rode on top of one of the golems as they marched the army to the Aurelian Empire.

They trod a tunnel through what Theira had come to think of as "her" forest. It would recover, and she would help, but part of her still ached at the sight.

Another part of her, though, burned.

Yes, her golem army—*their* golem army—would leave a mark.

Let them try to stop her now.

She was ready.

She'd *been* ready.

All she'd needed was Varius. Now he was with her, mind, body, and spirit.

And *no one* would take him from her.

Unless he himself decided to leave, but that was a different battle.

Now, they talked strategy for today.

Theira could animate the golems to march on her own, but Varius was still inside his. That way he was already armored, if they met resistance sooner than anticipated. And, frankly, given the noise a traveling group of giant clay soldiers made, they could hear each other more easily through her sorcerous array.

She missed the chance to touch him, but they both needed to focus.

With the vision he could access through the golems, Varius went grimly quiet as they approached the border of the Aurelian Empire.

The smoke was visible first. The fires, the shouting—closer now.

But since they were coming from Korossia, even amidst local unrest—perhaps especially amidst it—soldiers were still watching their direction.

The booming sound of the army's footsteps alerted the soldiers before they were in sight.

Sentries scurried, scouts ran ahead. Ran back even faster, sending up signal flares in case they didn't make it.

Show time.

A legion of Aurelian soldiers formed up on the border to meet them, a shield wall at their front even as smoke billowed behind.

"Theira," Varius said, "would you mind flying from here?"

Theira stood up on the golem's shoulder, playing with the light just a touch to make sure the soldiers saw her in her signature amethyst battle garb.

The Sorceress Transcendent, leading a sorcerous army straight at them.

The front held steady, because they knew it was their doom otherwise.

But at the back of the legion, the lines faltered.

At that, Theira launched into the sky.

And Varius took over controlling the golems.

Their gait shifted.

One step, two, three, and then with great booming crashes, the giants were running at a full sprint toward the Aurelian line.

When the golems reached the human legion, they blew through the front lines, and the rest collapsed behind in a stampede to get out of the way.

They had the advantage, but from there Varius' job grew more complicated. The more the soldiers spread, the more tasks he had to manage separately for the golems.

But mostly, he let them run.

He'd told her he'd focus on breaking the legion's resistance first, and only now did Theira understand that wasn't going to look like the kind of strategy she was used to from him. Breaking their resistance to the golems wasn't the same as breaking *them*.

Theira's role was different.

She surveyed the ground and chose her spot deliberately, letting her opponents come to her.

Because as *she* had expected, taking advantage of the chaos in the Aurelian Empire, a contingent of sorceresses had arrived.

Ten first-tier adepts. Tychon wasn't leaving this opportunity to chance.

That was... a more difficult problem than she'd anticipated. Theira over-prepared for every situation, but this would strain even her available resources.

A woman with brown hair and serious eyes greeted her. "First-Tier Adept Theira."

"First-Tier Adept Lysithea," Theira greeted her in return.

Unfortunate. Lysithea had always done the exact amount required of her and no further, its own kind of resistance. Theira respected her immensely, but Lysithea did not play games.

And she demonstrated it, bluntly stating, "Korossia thanks you for creating this opportunity. We are instructed to claim this ground. It is not our remit to take you in."

So Tychon was still mad, but he wouldn't let that cause him to miss this chance. And Lysithea would let her escape. That was a shocking endorsement, frankly.

But it only worked if Theira stood aside and let her own people invade the Aurelian Empire, as they'd been trying to do for decades.

Theira hadn't done all this just for the Sorcerer Ascendant to have more power.

"With regret I must decline," Theira said.

Lysithea's eyes narrowed, no doubt confused that Theira was deliberately refusing this extremely generous chance to escape Tychon's wrath. "It was not a request."

"And this is not an opportunity," Theira said, flinging a potion from her belt that detonated in the air and spread fire in a rush. Behind a wall of flames she said, "Not for Korossia."

The sorceresses snapped into action, and so did Theira.

She'd prefer not to kill Lysithea, as well as several others she'd thought also chafed under Tychon's rule, unlike Kryseia and her team. That made everything more complicated—especially if they noticed.

Maybe her role was like Varius' after all.

Fortunately, Theira could very easily make it look as though she was occupied just with trying to keep them from killing her.

The trick would be to *not*, in fact, let them exhaust her resources and kill her.

Varius was busy tearing a path of destruction through his own city. She'd told him she'd handle it, and he'd trusted her without question.

She couldn't back down now.

She *would* hold the line on her own.

Theira didn't hesitate, and reached for her own power.

Varius broke the lines of his own soldiers as he marched toward the city.

In his training with Theira, he hadn't needed to worry about damage. But he wasn't fighting sorcerers now; he was facing his own people.

Varius was glad he'd put some effort into learning how finely he could control the golems, because today, the challenge would be whether he could be careful enough.

Whether he could use his prodigious skill at destruction to free them, rather than just lead them into more death.

He didn't deserve forgiveness, but maybe he could avoid compounding his sins. Maybe he could even, finally, give them something that mattered.

Varius had won plenty of battles, but he had never been in a position to win a war.

The lines at the border had shattered, not even a token effort to reform, without the golems doing any more than approaching at speed. Whoever Sobanus had pressed into taking his place was either incompetent or a coward.

Considering he hadn't seen anyone wearing a legatus' helmet, he was guessing the latter.

That, or his soldiers had already taken matters into their own hands.

They'd abandoned all attempt at unified formation, but Varius was pleased to see a significant percentage of soldiers staying nearby, following his path. He kept the golems' pace even, allowing the soldiers to predict his movements and avoid them.

Varius wasn't here to sacrifice their bodies or trample their spirits. He had to find another way.

A conundrum, when the tool at his disposal was a giant sorcerous army.

But the continued presence of his soldiers gave him hope. They might not have wanted to fight the empire's wars, but they did want to protect their people. Some of them were even smart enough to notice that as long as they didn't stand in front of his golems, he ignored them.

His first step was clearly to circumvent dealing avoidable damage, but that wouldn't *fix* anything. He had all this power, but all he could do with it was break things.

Varius wielded tools of destruction, and maybe he couldn't build with them. But he could make space for others to, creating the structures and monuments that mattered in their lives.

Like Theira had.

And that meant daring to dream as boldly as she had, too.

So: since he had no interest in breaking his own people, what could he break? What *needed* breaking?

Power. Always, it came down to power.

And there were several ways he might break the power that mattered.

Maybe. If his years of service bought him anything, and if he played this just right.

So Varius cleared the streets of combatants.

But also of statues of patricians, by the simple expedient of swinging the golems' mighty arms, every crash more satisfying than the last, a rhythm building.

Advance.

Destroy.

Save.

That stone could be put to better purpose. The patricians didn't deserve veneration or even deference.

Varius directed the golems around buildings as much as possible, but some of the sturdier ones allowed the golems to pile on top of each other to scale them for better visibility through the smoke.

One golem he also pushed off a roof to shatter a particularly large effigy of Caius Sobanus.

Inexorably, the golems dispersed any remaining pockets of soldiers doing Sobanus' bidding and fighting against the citizens they had taken up arms to protect.

Some soldiers tried launching arrows, to see if they could even faze the golems, to no effect.

One brave contingent piled on a golem in an attempt to overwhelm it with numbers, which effectively blocked that one's vision but not all of them. Varius used another golem to, as gently as he could with giant clay fists, brush them off.

Still the soldiers tried to deflect this invasion on their city, launching fire.

Not stupid, and not giving up.

Until Varius used a golem to catch the fire and instead of hurling it back at them or just knocking it away into a building, he carefully set it in a fountain full of water, putting the flaming ballistic out safely.

And then his golem picked up a bucket of water and passed it to another, a line forming toward the center of a fire that only indestructible clay soldiers could get close enough to put out.

Watching that, finally, seemed to turn the tide.

Varius marched through the city, and gradually the soldiers followed him, fighting him less and less but keeping a careful eye on his progress. Eventually they formed lines to block certain routes difficult to see through the smoke. Varius recognized belatedly they were places the golems wouldn't fit, or that might be too structurally delicate to support their passage.

Maybe the soldiers suspected who was controlling the golems, but they didn't know. Did the deniability matter? And if they did know—

Varius couldn't let them down now. Not after how he'd left them, to this.

And the further Varius went, the less he recognized what the city had become.

But, of course, he did: the place he'd fought for so long to protect was now itself a battlefield.

It always had been, he realized. But not like this. Blood and rubble in the streets, screams of anguish rending the smoke-filled air.

By the time he reached the densest part of the inner-city action, soldiers within the city had broken into desperate segments as citizens hurled boiling pitch at them from behind houses, poured it from roofs.

Varius' pride in his people swelled. He'd reported on the tactics of sorcerous traps to the patricians, absolutely. But not only to them, and Aurelian citizens wouldn't simply lie down and take whatever Caius Sobanus thought they deserved.

He got his own golem between a barrage of pitch and soldiers, defending them. Then as the soldiers began to cheer their good fortune, he directed the golems toward them.

One step. Two.

The soldiers froze.

Varius almost did too.

Then he did what he always did: he steeled himself, and braced for impact.

And so he popped the top of his golem long enough to yell in an instantly recognizable voice that had carried over countless battlefields, "LEGIONS, DISPERSE!"

A beat, where he could practically feel their fear and confusion keeping them immobile.

And then his soldiers—*his* soldiers—the ones who'd followed him from the border, took matters into their own hands.

They didn't help their fellows reform a shield wall to deploy against the citizens.

They ran in and herded their compatriots away.

Following his orders, even now.

The only reason Varius didn't cry was his body was too caught up in the sorcery of managing a clay army.

An elderly woman with long gray hair, soot covering her hands and face, and an absolutely furious expression stepped out from behind a corner.

"Varius, you had better have a godscursed good explanation for this!" Fabiana hollered at him.

Ha! He knew it. Exultation filled him, relief fast on its heels.

They would be okay. With or without him, they would be okay.

Varius had been practicing with Theira, but it was hard to make a golem's bow ironic. He must have managed well enough, though, because the old woman snorted, scowled, and promptly snagged a passing soldier by the arm.

"You! Get started gathering the wounded."

The soldier froze—all of them did—turning as one to the golem Varius' voice had come from.

No help for it. At least he was wearing his armor this time.

Varius popped the top again, hauled himself up, and pointed at the soldier in question. "Do whatever the hell she says and thank her for the privilege. You destroyed this city, you will earn back the right to call it yours."

He cast his legatus stare—the one Theira had so recently mocked him for—around every soldier he could see.

Until, one after another, they saluted him.

Not forsaking him.

Theira wouldn't have done more than raise an eyebrow at him, but that was Theira.

Varius had too much experience ordering troops to clear his throat in front of them from emotion, but he was losing composure fast. How in the hells had Theira managed to keep it together swindling Tychon to his face not once, but twice?

He pointed to the old woman. "She has your marching orders now."

Every soldier turned in unison to her, pounding a fist on their breastplates. Instant willingness to following civilian leadership.

She just eyed Varius. "And you?"

"Tell me where to find Caius Sobanus," Varius said, his voice low and dangerous, "and I will end this."

No one moved.

Would they truly stand by a patrician of the empire against a sorcerous incursion, even after everything?

Would they truly and undeniably support *him*, even after everything?

"Legatus Varius, sir!" A voice finally yelled. "He is sheltered in the patricians' dome, sir."

Varius managed not to collapse as it felt like his bones lost all their strength beneath him in sheer relief, but it was a near thing.

It helped that his heart was pounding in anticipation, though.

The old woman shrugged. "That's what I would have guessed, too. Not like him to be seen anywhere a bit of dirt might touch him, is it?"

"Let's see," Varius said, "if I can't fix that."

He looked at the soldier who'd spoken; saluted. The man was ashen, but at this he glowed. Varius' chest constricted.

Maybe they didn't know what Varius had done to leave, or maybe they doubted what Caius Sobanus had told them before, or maybe—maybe they didn't blame him, for surviving. Maybe they recognized he'd been as caught as they were.

It had been too long since the soldiers of the empire could make a choice they felt good about. Varius had changed that, with Theira's help.

That was the answer to what he could offer them now.

A chance.

To make their own choices; to live.

He could break them all out of this cycle, once and for all, and he would.

Varius gathered the golems, and the rhythmic boom of their steps was as inexorable as the drum of the legions.

His soldiers ran ahead of him, removed any resistance. They took care of their own.

No soldier was loyal to the patricians who sent them to die over the legatus who'd saved their lives time and time again, who'd paid out his own money for their gear, who'd stood by their side to break news to their families.

Caius Sobanus' real mistake was believing his people were stupid.

Varius doubted he appreciated that, but soon it wouldn't matter.

As his golems closed in on the enormous stone dome, two soldiers carried a struggling Sobanus out.

"The patricians are inside, sir," one of them yelled up to Varius. "And only patricians, sir."

Well, well.

A perfect field for military exercises after all.

And a place where he didn't need to hold back his strength.

Varius approached in his own golem, reaching out to pluck Sobanus from between them and lifting him. The real trick was not to squeeze him to death.

With the golem's other hand, he pointed, and the soldiers got the hell out of the way.

He popped the top of his golem once more.

"You," Sobanus shrieked, "Traitor to the empire! You've marched against your own people—"

He broke off, choking, as Varius tightened his grip just a little.

"Only against you, Sobanus, and the ones who keep this war going."

The patrician said nothing, but his eyes were still furious, uncowed.

Caius Sobanus spat on the golem.

This wasn't a man who would learn anything. At least, not anything that mattered.

Varius felt responsible for his soldiers, and for the civilians in the city, but this? This was freeing.

"You wanted to know what would happen when you pushed me," Varius told him. "I invite you to watch."

Without waiting for a response, because nothing Sobanus could say had to matter to him anymore, he sealed himself back inside.

The golems surrounded the dome completely, like the shield wall of a legion.

And as one, they moved.

A boom with one step, as the ground shook.

A boom with the second, as their hands reached out as one.

This now, all of them together, was the easiest thing possible for Varius to do.

He forced sorcerous rock against an imperial hard place, and he pushed.

And he pushed, and he pushed.

Until the patricians' sanctuary, the seat of their power where now they cowered, shook.

In another moment, it began to crumble.

Varius kept pushing.

Loud cracks sounded, and inside, they would finally begin to understand what was happening.

A few men in the robes of patricians ran out screaming only to meet a wall of rock and be crushed underfoot.

The rest were silent as the stone dome collapsed on top of them.

Dust and debris from the force of the fall blew outward, blocking Varius' vision, but it too broke against the enormous stone soldiers.

When he could see again, Caius Sobanus was still held in his fist.

Varius wasn't sure if he was dazed or dead from the storm of the physical embodiment of his power physically collapsing to dust around him.

He also didn't care.

With one move, he smashed what remained of the man who'd sent Varius' own men after him into the rubble at his feet with such force that Sobanus was ignominiously pulverized against the stones.

No part of him was free from the dirt he scorned now.

Not a sound mourned his passing.

Varius took a breath. It was done.

His part was done.

A weight on his shoulders lifted, and he scarcely heard the cheers erupting around him.

He had already turned his sorcerous vision back to the border where he'd left Theira.

In time to see her take a hit from one of the *ten* god-scursed sorceresses that surrounded her.

Varius ran.

Theira was a whirlwind of power, throwing spell after spell, stemming the sorcerous tide of ten adepts at once, who at least even if they were fighting her at the same time weren't coordinating with each other, because sorceresses worked alone.

As much as Theira had been able to experiment since leaving Castle Korossia, and even more since she had Varius to play with, she had plenty of new tricks these sorceresses had never seen.

But improvisation was no substitute for advance planning, and she couldn't use much from the ground against them.

Theira threw a potion from her belt that swirled a poisonous miasma around her—sorceresses at her level dosed themselves against poison, so it wouldn't kill her or them, only slow them down while she figured out something more all-encompassing—

Lysithea's golden arrow speared through the cloud, hitting her in the side.

Theira gasped, the poison vanishing in an instant, and reflexively she threw bolts of magic like exploding a jar of marbles, forcing the sorceresses to dodge backward and giving her a moment to gather herself back together.

They'd realize quickly the drops of sorcery were nothing more than a feint to distract them.

Curse it. She couldn't use the ground, not now, but if she didn't—ten sorceresses were too many, even for her.

Varius' voice broke her focus. "Wait for me, Theira. I'm coming."

She *had* waited for him, and he *had* come. To her.

She wouldn't let him down now.

Theira was about to insist she had everything under control, when the sorceresses facing her stopped.

Stepped aside.

And the Sorcerer Ascendant himself walked through the chaos.

Tychon was power incarnate. Black robes billowed out behind him as he approached, each step reverberating through the earth from the mystical weight of Korossia's all-powerful Crown Jewel set atop a circlet on his head, radiating a malevolent magenta gleam.

"The Sorceress Transcendent," Tychon mocked her. "So accommodating of you not to run."

Lysithea's expression tightened. He'd known, as he always knew, what she would offer Theira, and Theira now understood why Lysithea had been shocked she hadn't taken the opportunity. She'd known, and assumed Theira knew, that the Sorcerer Ascendant was out for her blood. He'd only been waiting for a sign that Theira had spent whatever she'd prepared that had any teeth.

But Theira was done running.

"On second thought," Theira murmured to Varius, "I'm about to be very busy with one sorcerer in particular."

"I'm on my way," Varius said, and her heart warmed. The man was willing to put himself in the path of the most powerful sorcerer alive and go toe-to-toe with the best sorceresses Korossia could produce, for her. "Hold on."

"Oh," Theira said, and, knowing full well Tychon was listening, smiled wickedly, "I'm not waiting any longer."

And she moved, casting a dozen spells in an instant.

Tychon always waited for another sorceress to strike first, to demonstrate how little he had to fear from them, and today was no exception.

Today, that gave her a head-start, keeping him briefly occupied.

So she finally activated the spells she'd prepared on the ground.

Not today. There hadn't been time today.

But Theira had fought this war for a long time, and she'd laid spells *everywhere*. Places no one, even Varius, expected.

That was her greatest strength, after all. She prepared.

And she'd saved it all for just this moment.

She'd need every jot of that preparation now, her own internal resources depleted as she faced the full power of Korossia's Crown Jewel.

Theira scarcely noticed Varius arriving with the golems, repelling sorcerous attacks from two sorceresses at once. After all his practice with her, he could handle them.

The rest of the sorceresses had formed a wide circle around her and Tychon. Witnessing as they battled.

And oh, how they battled.

When she finally deployed the first spell she'd prepared, Tychon showed no surprise at her finally showing her hand.

He just smiled at her, a patronizing, condescending smile like he'd known all along what she had saved for him and had no concerns.

By Gaia, she'd change that.

Theira drew thunder and lightning from the earth beneath their feet to throw at him, her wild hair whipping around her, as Tychon batted them aside like flies and sent pure beams of magenta sorcery at her from the Crown Jewel. She raised defenses and he blasted them apart, but she was already in the air above.

His beams of power followed her, searing the sky, exploding buildings in the distance. Varius would have to use the golems to protect his people from becoming collateral damage, because Theira couldn't spare the attention.

She activated spell after spell, but nothing fazed Tychon or even blunted his attacks.

And little by little, Theira edged backwards as she bore up under his assault, her own internal resources already strained.

Little by little, she was losing.

The magenta sorcery of the Crown Jewel pierced her amethyst shield faster than she could dodge. Theira fell, already casting another shield even as she whipped a prepared potion off her utility belt to splash over the burn bubbling across her skin, the pain enough to register through her battle focus.

Now she wasn't a step ahead of him, but one behind.

The Sorcerer Ascendant gained ground. "You thought you could cheat *me*," Tychon said. "You thought you could leave. That you could be *free*." His voice mocked her. "Theira, Theira, Theira. My boldest little bee. You are mine to do with as I please, as you always have been."

His eyes burned with magenta fire.

"And today," he purred, "what I please is to crush you."

Finally, Theira stopped moving back.

It had to be here.

Tychon was almost to her—just a little farther—

He stopped his advance, smiling cruelly.

Theira's heart stopped, all her plans crumbling around her in an instant. *Did he know? Of course he knew, Gaia take it, he always knew --*

All her preparations, and she'd still failed. She wasn't going to make it after all.

Theira stood before the man she hated more than anything in the world, unmoving but unwilling to bow even now, as the Sorcerer Ascendant raised his hand for one final blow.

Then a golem crashed into him from behind.

Varius pushed Tychon forward that one final, crucial step.

Exactly where Theira wanted him.

Because as much as they'd fought together, even without Theira telling him the plan, Varius recognized her luring prey into a trap for what it was and had rendered the final assist.

Lines of power flared along the earth as the Sorcerer Ascendant stepped into the center of her most powerful spell and activated it.

Sorcerous vines wrapped around him, holding him in place, even as Tychon's magenta shields flared around him. The golem tried to hit him again and bounced right off, exactly as Theira's attacks had.

Tychon was furious. "You think you can win if you can just hit me? Go ahead, you fool. Nothing will reach me, and in a moment you'll regret your audacity."

It was Theira's turn to smile as she stepped closer. "No, I don't think I will."

Because the vines were already inside his shields, and now they sprouted thorns, piercing Tychon's skin.

Draining the power right out of him.

And into her.

As fast as the Sorcerer Ascendant could spend power, Theira's vines absorbed it, pumping the power straight into her depleted reserves.

She'd needed the space, after all.

This spell was the product of years of work and experimentation. Years of careful sneaking to the border to lay her spells in the ground in advance, which no one thought anything of, because it was war, and they knew how she fought.

They didn't realize she'd truly been fighting her war against Tychon.

Theira had a version of this spell in half a dozen places, unsure where exactly she would one day face Tychon. But this one, the closest to where she'd decided to make her home, this was the one she'd ultimately poured her power into in the period Varius had noticed her attacks growing more careful.

She was planning for her big moment to trick Tychon, true. But she'd laid those spells for longer.

This was what she'd been focusing on.

Now, she watched as Tychon realized with every moment he was only empowering her more.

"Kill Theira!" he yelled furiously at the other sorceresses, the ones Varius hadn't taken down, the ones who witnessed.

The sorceresses didn't move, and Theira's smile widened, a mad baring of teeth.

Of all people, first-tier adepts could recognize the way the wind blew.

Tychon snarled and began gathering his power for a single burst of sorcery that would explode off her vines.

Too late. He was out of practice fighting his own battles, relying on brute force, and it cost him.

Theira wasn't a sorceress who waited on others to make her move.

She took.

Before he could finish, Theira concentrated all the power thrumming through her into one narrow beam.

With a flick of her wrist, she sliced off the Sorcerer Ascendant's head.

Tychon's shocked face in the moment before his skull hit the ground was a beautiful sight she would cherish forever.

His severed head landed with an unremarkable thump. The circlet slipped off as Tychon's body disintegrated into dust.

Leaving Theira, flush with power, facing Varius in his golem and an army animated by her own sorcery behind him.

And eight now badly outclassed adept sorceresses around them.

As one, they sank to one knee and bowed before her.

The magenta jewel gleamed in the former Sorcerer Ascendant's ashes. Theira could feel it calling to her.

Hers to command, now. All the power in the world.

She'd won, and now she could end this war.

And she would.

Varius watched Theira consider the jewel before her, holding his breath as he fought to wait, to wait.

Theira always had a plan. He knew that in his bones, even if even he hadn't fully appreciated how far it had gone. But he'd known, if Theira was ever to be free, that the Sorcerer Ascendant would have to die, and she would have to kill him.

And he knew what killing the Sorcerer Ascendant meant for her.

Now she would become the Sorceress Ascendant herself. That was how she ended the war on the Korossian side.

"Sorceress Transcendent," Lysithea said, watching Theira closely, "will you return with us and take up your rightful place?"

Theira smiled widely. Delightedly, wickedly, and Varius practically felt his heart breaking.

Then she said: "No."

The very earth seemed to arrest in shock.

Varius didn't quite dare breathe.

Finally Lysithea echoed, faintly, "No?"

"Take the Crown Jewel with you if you wish." Theira shrugged, though she was taking clear pleasure in the very obvious shock she'd managed to pull from sorceresses trained in the most dangerous court in the world. "I will not take it up."

All at once Varius began to laugh, and laugh, and laugh.

Theira arched her eyebrows wickedly in his direction, and he allowed himself to breathe again, less hysterically.

Taking pity on the stunned-silent Lysithea, Theira told her, "I have no interest in ruling."

"But you killed the Sorcerer Ascendant! No one else can bind the jewel—" Lysithea's eyes widened.

"Exactly," Theira said with satisfaction. "I will not bind myself to the jewel, and if anyone else wants to become the Sorcerer Ascendant, they will first have to go through me. And I am not easy pickings."

She certainly wasn't. Not before, not with the power thrumming through her now, and not with what everyone finally understood of just how terrifying her skill at planning truly was.

And she'd held her own against ten first-tier adepts at once *without* that, only the spells and power she carried on her person.

One of the sorceresses protested, weakly, "You can't just do that?"

Theira raised a brow at her. "Oh? Do you intend to try to make me?" Her red lips curved, and she said mildly, "As ever, I am ready."

The sorceress paled and shook her head rapidly.

Lysithea asked, "So, what then? We just choose our own Ascendant?"

"Consider not choosing one," Theira suggested. "You have an opportunity to make a different way than at the whims of one omnipotent person in charge. Try something else."

"Just like that."

"Well, if I don't like what you decide on, I'll kill you. I *can* take up the Crown Jewel any time I want, after all. So put some thought into it."

For a woman who'd just been casually threatened by the most powerful sorceress alive, Lysithea looked overcome for quite a different reason.

All the sorceresses exchanged glances.

Cunning, yes, always.

But thoughtful.

And, Varius thought, in some of them, the seed of hopeful.

Theira was rescuing them after all, by giving them the opportunity to save themselves.

But then Lysithea said, "What you're suggesting will take work that we won't be able to focus on properly with this threat on our border."

"Entirely true," Theira agreed easily, and raised her eyebrows at Varius. "So?"

So? That's what she had to say to him?

This was ridiculous. Varius popped the top of his golem and heaved himself out, trusting Theira would protect him if it came to that.

"I don't speak for the Aurelian Empire," Varius said to the sorceresses with a speaking glance at Theira.

"You are commanding an invincible army and have just deposed the empire's local leadership rather extravagantly," Lysithea pointed out somewhat dryly. "Precisely who else would you suggest I address?"

Okay, that was fair. Succession in the empire was usually a matter of extremely corrupt election, but military takeovers weren't exactly unheard of.

But if he was in charge, Varius knew perfectly well how far he'd get if he tried to *keep* things as a military takeover.

So he said, "You should talk to Fabiana."

If Fabi didn't murder him for outing her, anyway. But with his golems' expansive vision he'd seen her clearly taking charge organizing the cleanup, so he was fairly sure her secret had come out with Sobanus' attack on the city even before he'd arrived.

All the sorceresses, Theira included, stared at Varius with varying degrees of expectation and incredulity. Well, they wouldn't have had any occasion to meet

Fabiana—though given how much time Theira had apparently spent on the wrong sides of borders undetected, the gods only knew whom she'd met.

Varius squinted, then pointed. "Theira, could you invite that woman to join us please?" He'd have to get back in the golem to do it himself.

The sorceresses stared between them. He could practically feel Lysithea trying to decide what exactly their relationship was, for two former enemies to address each other so casually.

"Gray hair, sending people scurrying one after another?" Theira clarified.

"That's the one."

"A moment."

Theira had one of the nearby golems lumber over to Fabiana, who squared her shoulders and held her ground while people dashed away. The golem kneeled before her and set an open hand on the broken pavement.

Fabiana put her hands on her hips and leaned around the golem. Varius waved at her, hoping that would be sufficient endorsement. Even without sorcerous vision he could feel her scowl, but she stepped onto the golem's palm and held on as it ran toward their position.

"No teleportation?" Varius asked.

Theira shrugged. "You said 'invite'."

So he had.

When the golem set her on the ground, Fabiana took a shaky step off and glared at him, then at Theira. "You used sorcery to cushion your ride over on one of those things, didn't you?"

That was Fabi all over. Never missing a detail, never afraid to demand answers, and practical to the bone.

Theira's lips curved. "Absolutely. Shall I craft a spell for your return?"

Fabiana snorted. "I'll walk, thank you. Why am I here, Varius?"

"Our Korossian neighbors have some questions about future Aurelian policy as it pertains to this border."

"Don't we all," Fabiana said. "Seems to me that's a you problem."

"And if you think I'm going to commit to anything without speaking to the head of the rebellion, you must think I've lost my wits."

"You *have* lost your wits, Varius, you came here with a bloody sorceress."

Her tone was tart, not accusing, so Varius said with some amusement, "Give me some credit, I did remove Sobanus for you."

"Remove, ha! We'll be scraping bits of him off the stone so we can rebuild."

Theira murmured, "A beautiful metaphor."

Fabiana snorted. "Are you asking for my backing, Varius, or my opinion?"

What *was* he asking her?

Varius regarded Fabiana, her brash behavior disguising the bone-deep fear she had to feel standing amidst all these sorceresses without any kind of military training or shield. And yet she hadn't hesitated, and wasn't letting on. She'd be a wonderful leader, given the opportunity.

Then he looked at Theira, who was watching him expectantly. Theira, who'd opened a new world of possibilities for him, a taste of a different way to live that he wanted so badly he *hurt*.

She'd refused to rule her country. She'd passed off that responsibility—mostly.

Maybe... maybe he could too.

Maybe not everything and everyone had to be his personal responsibility anymore. He *knew* they'd all benefit from someone outside the empire's power structure reshaping it.

Maybe, for once, he could dare to dream a little bigger—for his people, and for himself.

This, he finally realized, was actually what Theira hadn't wanted to tell him, before. It wasn't that she hadn't trusted him with her plan for Tychon.

It was that when the moment finally came to decide what kind of power he could wield, she didn't want to influence his choices. Didn't know if he would truly be happy turning his back on it all like she had, and was giving him the space to decide, without the weight of promises or expectations between them.

Theira was, as ever, doing her best—deniably, while making sure he had everything he needed—not to back him into a corner.

Varius had promised her he'd handle his side, and that didn't just mean his people.

It meant choosing for himself, finally, what he wanted. Like she had.

If he wanted a different life, one with her, he had to be the one to step up and claim it.

"I'm asking," Varius said slowly to Fabi, "if, with the patricians gone, you require immediate military support in order to take power yourself."

Fabiana frowned, her gaze searching his. "You want to be the power behind the throne? Again?"

Never. "I want to leave and never come back, Fabi. I'm asking if you need me to stay."

She raised her eyebrows in surprise, and then her gaze softened.

But Varius' heart sunk as her expression turned gentle.

"In a word, yes," Fabiana said. She glanced toward the sorceresses and back. "Our position isn't stable yet. If the empire sends legions from elsewhere, they'll roll over us. We need a champion that can make them back down."

Varius had bowed his head in resignation, but his mind kept spinning.

No. He wasn't ready to give up yet.

It was his turn to reach for a new life if he wanted it.

Wasn't he supposed to be a strategist? It was past time to apply that to his own life.

"Perhaps all you need," he said, turning to Theira, "is the *threat* of a champion."

Theira raised an eyebrow coolly, waiting.

She'd waited for him for too damn long.

"Would you object to leaving the golems here?" Varius asked. "As a deterrent."

"They won't do any good—or bad—without someone directing them. Only a fool won't put that together."

"We can make it known that Fabiana has a way to send a message to the house if needed."

Fabiana sucked in a breath. Lysithea and the other sorceresses held still, too.

Varius knew what he'd just implied, out loud and for an audience.

The only reaction he cared about in this moment was Theira's.

"You're sure?" she asked him softly.

"As sure as you don't want that jewel," he told her.

That wasn't all of what she meant, and he knew it, but *that* was a conversation for another, private, time.

Fabiana had missed the Crown Jewel part of the conversation, though, and this gave him an excuse to catch her up.

Theira didn't ask him again, letting the conversation move back to practicalities. She gave Fabiana a jewel that would send a message to the house, and Fabi promised to send updates. More rebels and disaffected soldiers joined them, and Varius tried to both reassure them but remain firm that he was absolutely not staying, no matter how much his now-aimless soldiers would love for him to. Theira engaged in quiet conversations with the sorceresses, too.

So Varius and Theira stood guard over the course of an afternoon as the sun began to set and Fabiana and Lysithea signed a nonaggression agreement and arranged for future communications. Varius moved the golems into position, forming a barrier around the border city—from Korossia and the rest of the empire alike.

And then, somehow, it was done.

The war was done.

Varius looked at Theira.

Theira looked at him.

Sorceresses, rebels, and soldiers all waited on them with bated breath.

Varius smiled.

Theira had opened the door for him.

It was on him to walk through it.

He held out a hand to her in invitation—then lowered it slowly toward the ground like the golem.

Theira's lips quirked, and she stepped forward, took his hand, and transported them both away.

In instant later, they stood in her forest.

Not the house.

Theira didn't wait. "I can make that message jewel connect to one that's portable. You don't have to stay at the house, though I'm sure their believing you're with me is an added deterrent."

He didn't misunderstand. She wasn't sure he'd still want her when they weren't bound together by circumstance and duty. He didn't assume that when she'd opened her door she'd meant it to be forever.

Varius squeezed her hand, and he also didn't wait.

No more. He'd already waited a lifetime.

"I want to stay at the house," Varius said. "I want to stay with *you*. If you'll have me."

Theira's eyes flashed with deep emotion, and she didn't answer right away.

But she stepped closer to him, and cupped his jaw with her free hand.

Varius pressed a soft kiss into it.

Theira purred, "And if I won't have you, Varius? What then?"

"I'll make a fantastic nuisance of myself," Varius teased. "Giving your garden all manner of challenge, which you know I can do even without a golem. Leaving strange objects on your doorstep to tempt you into opening the door—"

Laughing, she kissed him.

Varius wrapped his arms around her, full of her, and himself, and allowed himself to believe, for the first time, that he could be happy like this forever. They both could.

That was his new responsibility.

Walking through the forest was different now, hand-in-hand with the most powerful sorceress alive. Literally brighter, with the lingering daylight and the path the golems had cleared through the trees. Theira was too mentally tired from her battle with Tychon to do much for the forest now, and Varius was too braindead after controlling all the golems to do much more than let her lean on him, which he was happy to do forever.

But there was a hot cup of tea at the end of the road, and a bed, with the person he loved inside it.

At the sight of the house, Varius felt like he might burst. From hope, from rightness. From happiness.

Their house, now. His and Theira's.

To relieve the pressure in his chest, he asked Theira, "That hill above the Tridentis. How many explosive spells did you set up there, anyway?"

"*So many.*"

Varius erupted in laughter, the joy breaking free of the dam. He threw caution to the wind and said, "If you can dig some more clay out of the garden, I think I can fix that mug."

Theira cast a fond look at him. "Varius. Do you really think I *dug* all that clay for a golem army out of my garden?"

"Of course not," he said. "I figured you had to dig out the earth from below your house to put the reinforced level in, and then had an idea you had to try since you had all that dirt handy."

Theira's crack of laughter was the best music. "I'll make you all the clay you need." She paused and added, "My love."

Varius whirled to her and had them both on the ground in an instant, laughing and crying as he professed his love over and over and over.

No more waiting.

And on second thought, there were structural advantages to a golem-cleared forest, and perhaps—much later—he could persuade Theira to leave some of them: no sticks under their bodies, light to see his lover by, and no worries about breaking anything or activating defensive spells if the Sorceress Transcendent happened to release an uncontrolled burst of sorcery in the throes of passion.

There would be all the time in the world for that mug in their house later.

Next time.

Forever.

Thank You

Thank you for reading! This novella was a blast to write and just sort of erupted out of me. I hope you had even half as much fun reading as I did writing it.

If you enjoyed reading *The Sorceress Transcendent*, please consider telling someone about it or leaving a review! Reviews are the lifeblood of any author, helping new readers find their next read.

For a FREE, newsletter-exclusive bonus epilogue, *sign up for my newsletter at caseyblair.com*! Subscribing will keep you in the loop on free fiction opportunities, sales, and new books.

You can also join my extremely low-key reader group on Discord where we share book recommendations, cat pictures, and sneak peeks of my works in progress.

Happy reading!

Casey

NEWSLETTER STORY

Get multiple FREE, exclusive short stories when you sign up for my newsletter at caseyblair.com, including **a steamy bonus epilogue for** *The Sorceress Transcendent*!

This short story takes place exactly one year after the events of *The Sorceress Transcendent*, with Theira and Varius trying their best to take care of each other on the anniversary of their reunion in… different ways.

Spoilers, it is NOT fade-to-black / closed-door. =)

THE SUNDERED REALMS

Liris has always been too dangerous to be allowed freedom. Now she's the universe's only hope.

Liris has been trapped training as an elite spy her whole life. But when her elders try to sacrifice her to further their own interests, she escapes through a secret portal—only to land right in the hands of Lord

Vhannor, the most dangerous spellcaster in the universe.

Vhannor has dedicated his life to defending the universe from world-devouring demons, and Liris, with her unique knowledge of an ancient spell language, jeopardizes his mission. But when she uses it to help him close a demonic portal before it can destroy all life in that dimension, he's forced to acknowledge he needs her by his side.

As they race between dimensions to fight their mutual enemies, they discover a plot that will leave every remaining realm in the universe at the mercy of demons. But to stop it, Liris will have to rely on the man whose icy gaze sees right through her... and when even her own people betrayed her, how can she trust Vhannor to stand by her when she risks the whole universe?

The Sundered Realms is equal parts epic fantasy and romance in a world where being a huge nerd about language makes you incredibly epic at magic. This is an action-packed story about an interdimensional combat ambassador heroine and the most dangerous man in the universe devoting all his attention to making her unstoppable.

ALSO BY

Diamond Universe: Sierra Walker
Take Back Magic
Take Back Demons
Take Back Worlds

Sundered Realms
The Sundered Realms

Tea Princess Chronicles
A Coup of Tea
Tea Set and Match
Royal Tea Service

Tales from a Magical Tea Shop:
Stories of the Tea Princess Chronicles

Stand–Alone
The Sorceress Transcendent
Consider the Dust

About the Author

Casey Blair is a bestselling author of hopeful fantasy novels about ambitious women who dare, including the Diamond Universe, Sundered Realms, and Tea Princess Chronicles series. Her own adventures have included teaching English in rural Japan, taking a train to Tibet, rappelling down waterfalls in Costa Rica, and practicing capoeira. She now lives in the Pacific Northwest and can be found dancing spontaneously, exploring forests around the world, or trapped under a cat.

For more information visit her website casey-blair.com or follow her on Instagram @CaseyLBlair.